Second Term  at L'Etoile

School
for
Stars

Also by Holly and Kelly Willoughby

First Term at L'Etoile

Second Term at L'Etoile

School for Stars

Holly & Kelly Willoughby

Orion
Children's Books

First published in Great Britain in 2013
by Orion Children's Books
a division of the Orion Publishing Group Ltd
Orion House
5 Upper St Martin's Lane
London WC2H 9EA
An Hachette UK Company

3 5 7 9 10 8 6 4

ISBN 978 1 4440 0813 5

www.orionbooks.co.uk

Printed and bound in Great Britain by Clays Ltd, St Ives plc

For girls who make the best of friends;
for girls who are inspired to achieve their dreams;
for girls who then go on to inspire others;
for girls who go on to become mothers.

Contents

Welcome back, dear Story-seeker, to this second term at L'Etoile.

We're so happy to have you with us once again, to share in the life and times of Maria, Molly, Pippa and their friends. There's so much gossip to catch up on from the Christmas holidays, and so many adventures ahead.

Are you ready? I know we are.

Love,
Holly and Kelly Willoughby x

1

L'Etoile, Sweet L'Etoile

'Molllly!' Maria shouted to her sister. 'Would you please shut that window – it's like an iceberg in here.'

Reluctantly, Molly tumbled backwards onto her bed, slamming the window shut as she fell.

'Where on earth can she be?' Molly groaned. 'I can't believe it's been nearly a whole month since we've seen our lovely Pippa. Barbados was *amazebells* and all that, but a bit last minute and I would far rather have had some fun at home with her.'

'Don't be so ungrateful, Moll,' Maria snapped. 'Do you know how many girls dream of having a holiday like the one we've just had?'

'I know, I know – I just miss her, that's all. Plus, I can't wait to give her her Christmas present.' Molly undid the bow on the little red box for about the tenth time since they'd arrived back at L'Etoile that morning, to admire the little gold star necklace engraved with a 'P'. 'She's going to absolutely love it!'

'I have to agree there, Moll. Mum really does have the best taste ever and the fact that all three of us have one, the same little L'Etoile star – each with our initial on – makes it all the more special.'

'I know! M, M and P. BFFs! It was such a shame Pips couldn't come and stay with us over Christmas but, like Mum said, hopefully this necklace will make up for us doing a disappearing act for the whole break.'

'Yo! Anyone ho-ome?' came an excited voice from the corridor. All at once, the door burst open and Pippa appeared, loaded with bags and sporting her best attempt at a posh 'hair up' do to impress Miss Molly.

'Pips!' Molly shrieked, launching herself at Pippa, knocking her backwards into the corridor. 'And you've done your hair! Very sophisticated.'

'What a welcome,' Pippa giggled, delighted her efforts hadn't gone unnoticed. 'Oh, girls. I've missed you so much! Can't wait to hear all your news.'

'What took you so long?' asked Molly. 'It's typical. I've been watching for you out of the window for the last hour – and then the second my back is turned, you show up!'

'It's like I told you, Molly – what is that saying about a watched pot never boiling?' said Maria with a grin.

Pippa and Molly both gave her their very best 'put-a-sock-in-it' look.

'So come on then, tell me . . . what's the goss?' Pippa asked, as she dragged her case onto the bed and started to unpack.

'I don't know where to begin,' Maria answered. 'Have you been keeping up with the *Yours, L'Etoilette* blog while we've been on hols?'

'Yes. I loved all your backstage blogs about the Christmas gala, but all of that was mainly school stuff – what's new with you two? I want to hear about all the latest Fitzfoster twin shenanigans since we said goodbye,' said Pippa.

'Ha! OK. But first things first – is it present time, Mimi?' Molly asked Maria desperately.

'I can't believe you've waited this long!' Maria said and then turned to Pippa. 'It's just a little something from Mum . . . erm . . . and us, to say happy Christmas and so sorry you couldn't come and stay with us. Mum felt so guilty for having to cancel our sleepover, she bought us all matching presents!'

Molly dragged Pippa over to sit on her bed and handed her the little red box with the bow, now frayed and untidy from too much tying and untying. 'Mum said it's so we can always feel close to one another, even when we are apart.'

Pippa was intrigued. 'Oh, but I haven't bought you girls anything. You shouldn't have . . .' Pippa was speechless when she saw the beautiful gold star necklace glittering up at her, with the letter 'P' inscribed in the centre. 'Oh my goodness, I love it!' she exclaimed. 'I don't think I've ever had anything so gorgeous! Thank you soooo much, girls. Quick, Molly, will you put it on for me?'

Molly was on cloud nine. In some way, getting the right gift for someone who loved it was far more fun than receiving one.

'Look, Pips – we all match now.' The twins held out their stars, both inscribed with the letter 'M', for her to see.

'I just don't know what to say. Really, thanks a million, girls. This means the world to me,' Pippa said, clutching it tightly.

'And I have a little something for you too, Pips,'

Maria said, handing over a silver DVD. 'I would have posted it to you over Christmas but didn't get a chance to download it before we went away.'

'What is it?' Pippa asked.

'It's a recording of your performance at the Christmas gala . . . so you can show your mum and Uncle Harry. Maybe it'll go some way to make up for them not being there for your big moment.'

'You're kidding me! I can't believe it. Is there anything you girlies haven't thought of?' Pippa said, turning the disc over and over in her hands. She couldn't wait to show her family – and to watch it back herself. 'Ooooh, I love you girls! What a welcome! Right, now it's my turn,' she said, rummaging around in her music bag.

'What have you lost?' Molly asked, excitedly.

'Ah ha! Here it is. Actually, this can be my Christmas present to you two,' Pippa said, sliding a CD into the player. 'While you were sunning yourselves in the Caribbean, I spent pretty much every day of the holidays in the studio with Uncle Harry, working on some new songs. And here's one I wrote for you both. It's called "Friends Forever".' She pressed play and the song burst out of the speakers.

Ooooh . . . just little old me,
Ooooh . . . then we were three.

I can't explain the feeling,
The one that leaves me reeling.

I never thought that friends could be
A second kind of family,

Ooooh . . . this ain't no short-term endeavour
Oooooh . . . you know we're friends forever . . .

The L'Etoilette trio sat bobbing their heads to the beat, grinning from ear to ear as the track continued to play.

'It's BRILLIANT!' exclaimed Maria and Molly in unison as it finished.

'I just don't know how you do it. And I love the lyrics . . .' Molly began singing at the top of her voice:

Ooooh . . . just little old me,
Ooooh . . . then we were three.

'Well, if you've picked it up that quickly – at least we know it's catchy,' Pippa beamed, loving the twins' response to all her hard work.

Knock, knock.

'Who is it?' Maria called out.

A voice boomed through the door, making them jump. 'L'ETOILETTES, WOULD YOU PLEASE KEEP THE NOISE DOWN!'

Who on earth was that? All of a sudden, Sally Sudbury thrust open the bedroom door, which hit the wall with a crash.

'SALLY!' Molly cried with delight. 'Sally, Sally – so good to see you. You look great. I love your boots – so this season! How are you?'

'Really, Molly? Thanks!' Sally said as she hugged the girls, delighted her Christmas-present footwear was a hit with the queen of fashion. 'I'm good, thanks . . . really good, as a matter of fact. Guess what?' she almost burst with excitement, 'Lucifette's not coming back to L'Etoile this term!'

'WHAT?' Maria, Molly and Pippa gasped with glee.

'Now *that* is what I call a Christmas present!' Maria joked.

'Oh, Sally – that's wonderful news. Quick – grab a fairy cake,' Molly pointed to a box of half-eaten homemade cakes on the bed. 'And tell us everything!'

Sally sat down and took a deep breath. 'You should have seen her after the gala. Boy, was I ever in the wrong place at the wrong time. Stupidly, I stayed backstage after I'd done my poem because I wanted to witness her get busted – but I didn't think far enough ahead to realise I would be the first person she'd run into as she came off stage! Honestly, she was in that much of a rage, I thought she was going to knock me out!'

'Oh, Sally, you poor thing. But by the way, your poem was simply wonderful. I didn't get a chance to say after the show. You're so clever,' Pippa said, and then realised she was changing the subject too soon. 'Sorry – do carry on – then what happened?'

'Oh, thanks so much! I'd quite forgotten that went so well with everything that's happened since,' Sally said. 'Anyway, as you can imagine, she was furious and mortified about being caught out like that in front of everyone. She was ranting and raving at such a pitch all the way to the car, I couldn't even understand what she was saying. I thought she was going to bust a vocal chord!'

'Hoped she would, you mean,' chuckled Maria.

'No such luck. It wasn't a pretty sight. As you know we didn't even go back to the dorm to get our bags. Miss Coates had to pack them and give them to the courier the next day. Mr and Mrs Marciano wouldn't hear of us going back to Garland. They couldn't bear the humiliation of having to see anyone after the show – for Lucifette – or themselves! So we were whisked straight off to London. From what I gather, the Marcianos sent a fairly large cheque for the L'Etoile Founder's Fund – to try and smooth over the embarrassment.'

'Well, they do say money talks,' said Pippa.

'Yes and Lucifette's walked!' said Maria, excitedly. 'So, is she gone for good, Sal? And, more to the point, how did you manage to get them to let you come back to L'Etoile by yourself? I should have thought Lucifette would have needed to bully you more than ever after what happened.'

'Well, that's the funniest part!' Sally said. 'That family is so arrogant, Mrs Marciano actually said as part of my punishment – for not somehow preventing the situation – I was to come back to L'Etoile on my own rather than having the honour of being by her daughter's side!'

'How lucky is that!? You're going to have the time of your life this term, Sally. You'll feel free for the first time in years I should think,' Molly said. 'And judging by the fact you're still breathing, I'm guessing they don't know you helped expose Lucifette then?'

'Oh, don't. In actual fact, for a minute I thought she might have realised that I was the only other person who knew the whole story to betray her. But luckily she thinks I'm too stupid to think for myself. She's put the whole thing down to Pippa chickening out of the fake Universal Music audition.'

'Oh, great!' said Pippa. 'So I am public enemy *numero uno*. Just tell me she's not coming back – ever!'

'Sadly, we're not that lucky. She managed to talk the Marcianos into letting her spend a term at a special acting school in LA. She's aiming to be back next term so she can sit the end-of-year exams and pass with flying colours.'

'Well, that's something to look forward to then,' said Maria sarcastically.

'What? Lucifette coming back – or end-of-year exams?' groaned Molly. 'Just listen to us!' she continued. 'Let's focus on the positives and be happy for now that we've got a whole term without her. Think how deliciously uneventful it's going to be.'

But as we know, Story-seeker, those are famous last words. Life is never quite what you expect it to be!

2

One Hundred Years of L'Etoile

'Welcome back, L'Etoilettes, to this, our first assembly of the spring term. I trust you have all had a good rest over the Christmas period and that you haven't eaten too many mince pies.' Madame Ruby raised an eyebrow at the students. Only Sally winced at the mention of mince pies. Her mum really was the best cook on the planet.

'The aim this term is for you all to build upon the strong foundations you laid before Christmas, so that you will excel in the third-term examinations.'

A muffled groan rippled round the Kodak Hall. Madame Ruby flashed a red lipstick smile at the

♥ 11 ♥

students. Why did teachers always seem to relish the pain of exams?

'I do, however, have one piece of news, which will be exciting for you to hear. As some of you may know, Friday 28th February will mark our 100th Founder's Day and, to celebrate, I have arranged something so special, I can hardly believe it myself.'

As she looked around the hall, she noted how she had the complete attention of everyone present – just the way she liked it.

'This year we will not only have the usual key entertainment industry figure as Founder's Day speaker, but we will be honoured to have a member of the Royal Family in attendance, to present a select few students with some special Centenary Celebration Awards.'

A gasp went up from the girls, followed by excited chatter and speculation as to which royal member Madame Ruby might be talking about.

'Ladies, please, I require your attention a moment longer. I know you will all be desperate to know *who* it is, however, I have been sworn to secrecy by Buckingham Palace officials, as a matter of national security. It is essential, for the safety of the royal in question, that his or her visit be kept under wraps until the very last moment. My only assurance to you is that he, or she, is one of the high-ranking, younger members of the Royal Family.'

That was enough to send the assembled audience into orbit. There were two young princes – one, the newly married heir to the throne, and then his handsome, single, younger brother. Could L'Etoile be any more wonderful?

'After His, or Her, Royal Highness has presented the Achievement Awards to the selected students, I would like us to show our appreciation in the form of some outstanding entertainment. After all, that is our forte, L'Etoilettes! In order to decide who will perform, I would like each year to prepare and select three solo or group pieces, to present to me at the end of the month. I will then choose one winning entry from each year group, so that we may display something worthy of a royal audience.'

As the girls began to clap and cheer, Madame Ruby put up her hand for silence and continued, 'Weather permitting, our L'Etoile Centenary Founder's Day celebrations will be brought to a close with fireworks at sundown by the lake.'

And with a triumphant nod, Madame Ruby swooshed off the stage leaving her audience applauding as if they were under some kind of spell.

'I just can't believe it,' said Molly as they filed out of the hall. 'It's just TGTBT!'

'TGTBT, Molly?' asked a dumbfounded Pippa. She'd quite forgotten about Molly's habit of abbreviating words.

'Too good to be true, Pips,' Molly grinned. 'I mean, a real live, up close and personal, introduction to one of the royal princes. This truly is what dreams are made of.'

'Wouldn't be so sure it is one of the princes,' Maria pointed out. 'The Queen does have other grandchildren you know. It could easily be one of the young cousins.' But Molly wouldn't hear of it. She had every faith that Madame Ruby, for all her faults, wouldn't settle for second best. 'Well, you think what you want to think Mimi, but my money's on it being handsome Prince Henry. You just wait and see!'

'Oooh, do you really think so, Molly?' Belle Brown asked, overhearing the twins. 'Wouldn't that just be the best thing ever to happen in the history of the whole world?'

As Form 1 Alpha readied themselves for their first history class of the term, everyone was talking about Founder's Day.

'Doesn't your mum work at the palace, Amanda?' Daisy, the bassoonist, asked the dancer.

'Not any more,' Amanda answered. 'She has a new job working for the Prime Minister at Number 10, but she might still be able to find out some insider info. I'll phone her as soon as I can tonight.'

'Well so long as there's an HRH in front of their name, I'd be 'appy to meet any member of the Royal Family!' Alice, the cockney car-park-heiress joined in. 'I fink I might faint though if I actually had to speak to one.' The class giggled, all picturing lovely, but clumsy Alice attempting a wobbly courtsey.

Maria was busy scribbling down notes for her first *Yours, L'Etoilette* blog of the term. She'd made two columns – the first listed the points Madame Ruby had made that morning and the second was a to-do list of all the things she needed to research. Things like some background on the history of L'Etoile and its founder. The only thing she knew about it was that it had been founded by Madame Ruby's great-grandmother, Lola Rose D'Arcy, and that there was a huge oil portrait of her hanging above the fireplace in the entrance hall of L'Etoile.

'Good morning, girls,' said Mrs Butter – or 'old Butter-boots' as the girls had nicknamed her, as she insisted on wearing the same yellow wellies, day in day out, come rain or shine.

'Good morning, Mrs Butter(-*boots*),' the class sang sweetly back to her.

The boots part, of course, said under their breath. Story-seeker.

'So lovely to see you all looking so refreshed after the holidays. And I see you've bought this term's study books – very well done indeed. But for our first few lessons together Madame Ruby has instructed me to teach you a short history of L'Etoile, in preparation for the Founder's Day Centenary festivities.'

Bless old Butter-boots, Pippa thought. She didn't think she'd ever met anyone so enthusiastic about life.

Maria was, of course, delighted. It was as if her mind had been read. This would save her valuable, swotting-up-in-the-library time and probably mean that she could upload her first blog of the term before lights out that night.

In fact all the girls were more attentive than usual. They were keen to know more about the event that would lead to an audience with a prince.

Old Butter-boots finished rummaging around in

her bag and pulled out some slightly dog-eared fact sheets, which she handed to Lydia, the cellist, to pass around.

'L'Etoile School for Stars, was the brainchild of Lola Rose D'Arcy,' she began, pushing her spectacles down the bridge of her nose, so that she could peer over them at her class.

'Lola Rose was a beautiful, creative, wealthy widow and mother to one little girl, Eliza Rose. After her husband passed away, she bought the L'Etoile estate from Lord Wilton in the early 1900s, with the intention of transforming it from the huge family home it had been since it was built in 1800, to the fabulous, functional school building you see today.'

Molly gazed around the room, with its high ceilings and towering sash windows, and let her imagination run wild, picturing the Wilton family going about their daily life.

'Once the proud owner of the estate, it took Lola Rose another seven years to research and find the perfect architect to take on the project of transforming it into her vision. Eventually, she learned of a man by the name of Frank Hart, who was at that time working on an important commission for the Royal Family of Monaco at one of their palaces. You might think that Lola Rose was being a bit too fussy, but from the minute she met Frank Hart and discussed her hopes and dreams for the school with him, she felt he was so in tune with her vision, it just had to be him. Sadly, this meant waiting another two years for him to finish the project in Monaco.'

'Oh, Miss. Do you think she fancied him, Miss?' asked Alice.

Mrs Butter smiled sweetly. 'It's funny you should pick up on that, Alice, dear. In actual fact, there were rumours of a romance between Frank and Lola, but nothing was ever known for sure.'

As the class continued to listen to the history of the school, how the buildings were extended and new parts like the Kodak Hall added one by one, Maria had become obsessed by the mention of a potential *love affair* between their founder and her architect. *This was it!* she thought. This was the interesting route her research could take for the blog. She, Maria wannabe-hot-journalist Fitzfoster, would uncover the truth about this couple and *Yours, L'Etoilette* would report back with the facts!

3

The Legend of the Lost Rose

'Here, listen to this, Moll,' Maria whispered from under her duvet.

'Oh, what now?' Molly grumbled, sleepily. 'Can't you put that laptop away, Mimi, it's gone ten o'clock. I'll never get up in the morning.'

Maria had been up very late finishing her first blog, entitled, *Will The Prince be Charming?* but still thought she'd do a little extra research of her own.

'I know it's late, and I'm sorry, but you know I can't sleep when I get a bee in my bonnet! I've been trawling the internet for hours now trying to find something on Frank and Lola Rose, and hadn't found a single scrap of info . . . until this,' she whispered excitedly.

'Go on then – but bring it over here. You always skip bits if you're tired. I need to read it myself,' Molly said, throwing back the covers to make space for her sister.

As Maria got up, Pippa flicked the lamp on. 'What are you two up to? Don't you dare go leaving me out of this,' she said, leaping over to Molly's bed too. 'I've been desperate for a bit of adventure all holidays!'

'Sure!' Maria said. 'The power of three is a whole lot better than the power of one. Budge up, Moll.'

The happy trio huddled together for warmth and began reading an article Maria had uncovered, by hacking into the *London Gazette* newspaper archives. The piece was written by a journalist hilariously named Luscious Tangerella and, for some reason, had been removed from normal public access.

'I'm going to have to think up a fake journalist name for myself. Maria Fitzfoster seems so dreary compared to the exotic Miss Tangerella!'

'Shush, Mimi – how can we possibly concentrate if you keep talking!' Molly snapped.

Maria smiled at her sister, and mimed fixing an imaginary padlock to her lips and throwing away the key.

'Give it here, I'll read it out.' Pippa grabbed the laptop from the squabbling twins.

THE LONDON GAZETTE

THURSDAY 10TH FEBRUARY 2000

The Lost Rose of L'Etoile, School for Stars

One could hardly deny the force of attraction between the wealthy widow, Lola Rose D'Arcy and her architect, Frank Hart. It was undeniably love at first sight, but out of respect for their departed spouses, it was a love which was always to be observed from afar. There was a mutual respect and adoration for each other, which was never to be anything more than friendship.

'How heartbreaking,' sighed Molly. 'Just like Romeo and Juliet.'

Pippa continued:

If that wasn't enough sadness for one couple, true tragedy struck when Lola Rose died unexpectedly of influenza a mere two weeks before work on her beloved L'Etoile was finished, and the school was due to open. It was no secret that Frank Hart was unable to hide the depth of his despair. It was rumoured that he had been on the verge of proposing to Lola Rose, but alas, they were never to have that their happy-ever-after ending. The story goes that Frank cleared the estate of workers on the day of her memorial service, so that he could be alone with the memory of his lost love, and that while there, he hid one of his most precious possessions somewhere on the L'Etoile estate, as a gift to her. That night, he died in his sleep, apparently from a broken heart. The secret location of his hidden treasure has never been revealed.

As years have gone by, the story has become a legend. The Legend of the Lost Rose of L'Etoile remains, to this day, one of the most intriguing, unsolved, local mysteries. I guess the question you have to ask yourself is, do you believe in fairytales?

Molly had tears running down her cheeks. 'I can't bear it. How much sadness can one family take?'

'Two families you mean!' Maria exclaimed.

'Shhhhh!' Molly and Pippa both warned.

'Sorry,' Maria whispered. 'It's just too exciting for words. You see, there's more. I found another website, which pieces together family trees, and look what else I've discovered.'

She clicked open another article and the trio scanned Lola Rose D'Arcy's family tree and Frank Hart's family tree. As they read the names of each generation, they couldn't believe their eyes.

'It turns out,' Maria went on, 'that there was some covenant in Lola Rose's will, that should anything happen to her, the D'Arcy family would always do right by the Hart family, giving them a roof over their heads and gainful employment, for as long as L'Etoile still stood.'

'So let me get this right,' Molly breathed, incredulous. 'Frank Hart had a son called Freddie Hart who became the first in a line of 'Hart' caretakers at L'Etoile. Freddie then had a son called David Hart who had a daughter called . . .'

THE D'ARCY LINE

Lola Rose D'Arcy
m. Benjamin D'Arcy (widowed)

|

Eliza Rose D'Arcy
m. Calum Yarwood

|

Amber Rose Yarwood
m. Nicholas Rees

|

Ruby Rose Rees
(never married, but chose to keep the
D'Arcy name of her great-grandmother)

THE HART LINE

Frank Hart (widowed)

m. Sophie Brooks

|

Freddie Hart

m. Olivia Buch

|

David Hart (widowed)

m. Alexandra Battle

|

Helen Hart

(Helen's mother died in childbirth. Helen was a
good ten years or so younger than Madame Ruby.
Madame Ruby's mother, Amber Rose D'Arcy,
doted on Helen as though she was her own.)

'Helen Hart!' Pippa exclaimed, with a gasp.

'Sshhhhhh!' the twins grinned at Pippa.

'Sorry . . . Helen Hart,' she repeated in a whisper.
'Oh my goodness, it all makes sense now. So Miss
Hart literally grew up at L'Etoile, as kind of a kid
sister to Madame Ruby, with her father, David Hart,
the caretaker. Wow – no wonder Madame Ruby is
so overfamiliar with Miss Hart and treats her like a

little sister – the adopted little sister she never wanted and was forced to share her life with. And we already know Miss Hart attended L'Etoile as a student – I can't imagine how resentful Madame Ruby must have been about the caretaker's daughter getting the same education she did. As much as she goes on about the importance of scholarships, and everyone having equal opportunities to develop their talents regardless of their financial background, there is a part of her which seems to resent it. Take me, for instance; she could hardly look me in the eye at the Christmas gala, when everyone else was so kind and positive about my performance. I think she would have much preferred the Hollywood princess, Lucinda, to steal the show over little old me! In a way, I probably remind her a bit of Miss Hart.'

'And you probably remind Miss Hart of Miss Hart!' said Maria, fondly. 'I know who I'd rather have fighting my corner. She adores you, Pips.'

'Well done, Mimi! You've uncovered more facts in the last few hours than a lifetime of old Butter-boots' history lessons.'

'Ah thanks, girlies,' said Maria, blushing. 'But you're right Moll, it's really late now. We really should get some sleep or we'll never get up in the morning.'

'Totes agree!' whispered Molly. 'Our minds need to be razor sharp to solve this little mystery!'

The exhausted trio clambered back into their own beds, each hoping their dreams would be filled with ancient maps and lost treasure.

4

A Very Happy Distraction

'*Y*ou know, I was thinking, Mimi, it's a good job you had to hack into the *London Gazette* archives to access that report. Can you imagine the competition we'd have trying to solve this mystery if the rest of the school could access that info easily and knew about *The Legend of the Lost Rose?*' Molly said to her sister, after almost a whole week without any new clues.

Maria was barely listening. The frustration of hitting dead end, after dead end, was killing her. She couldn't even be bothered to blog – which was creating havoc with the school rumour-mill. There were all sorts of stories going around about the student behind *Yours,*

L'Etoilette having been discovered by the teachers and expelled. But that was the least of Maria's worries. She simply had to get some answers – or at least another lead to follow up on soon.

As luck would have it, Story-seeker, a happy distraction arrived courtesy of Molly's weekly fashion delivery driver, Albie Good.

'Pips – do you want to come with me to meet Albie this afternoon?' Molly asked one Friday, not daring to ask miserable Maria.

'Love to – when's he coming?' Pippa answered.

'He's just sent me a text saying he's running a bit late – mentioned having to see a man about a dog or something. Goodness only knows what goes on in that boy's life. Anyway, he should be here just after individual music study. I'll meet you in the usual place behind the caretaker's shed halfway up the drive.'

'Perfect!' said Pippa, running off to class.

Albie Good was one of the girls' favourite people. He'd been instrumental in the rescue operation which had brought poor Pippa back from that disastrous trip to London, before Christmas.

Today was Friday, or 'Albieday' as it was now known and Albie was making his way to L'Etoile with Molly's latest fashion delivery and any odds and ends her parents wanted to send down for their daughters – usually the latest gadget or gismo Maria had begged for to assist her with her journalistic work. Molly had put in such a huge order in the January sales on *www.looklikeastar.com*, she'd been literally marking the days off her calendar waiting for Friday to arrive. It would be like Christmas all over again. She was particularly proud of the three fluffy white dressing-gowns she'd ordered for herself, Maria and Pippa, each embroidered with their names on the back so they didn't get muddled up. They'd come in so handy during those cold midnight chats when there were important issues to be discussed! She was a bit worried that Albie wouldn't be able to fit everything on the back of his bike and that he might have to save some of the stuff to bring down later. *Pleeeease don't let it be the dressing-gowns and those new Hollywood Curl hair tongs* she thought. She couldn't wait to get her paws on Pippa's crazy locks again.

Albie always looked forward to this part of the week
– but today he was distracted. When he'd said he had
to see a man about a dog, he hadn't been joking. He
honestly had been to see a man about a dog. Or to be
more specific – a beautiful, black, Labrador puppy.

As Albie waved to Molly and Pippa, and started to
slow his bike, the girls spotted a little black ball of fur
jump out of the sidecar and come hurtling towards
them.

'Moll . . . did you see . . . what on earth . . .' Pippa
almost got her question out, before Molly was leapt on
by an adorable, panting pooch.

'Oh puppy dog! Hello puppy, hello!' she cried,
burying her head in the soft black fur as the puppy
licked her face all over. 'Oh, Albie, it's so cute!'

Albie, also panting, had thrown down his bike,
ignoring the fact that his precious parcels were getting
soggy on the wet lawn as he ran towards the girls.

'Sorry, Miss Moll. I just don't know what to do with her. She's so naughty!' Albie stammered, clearly furious with the little dog.

Molly covered the puppy's ears. 'Oh puppy! Don't you listen to that mean Albie Good. *Albie Bad* more like! How can you be naughty when you're so sweet?'

'Come on, Albie – spill the beans. What's with the dog?' Pippa teased.

'There's nothing dodgy about her, Miss Pippa, honest,' Albie said. 'I rescued her. One of the boys at the warehouse came in with a box full of stray puppies on Monday, saying they'd have to be put down if he couldn't find homes for them by the end of the day. I asked Dad if I could keep one at the flat, but he said no. You know I've always wanted a dog, so I was gutted. But when the end of the day came, and I saw that there were no takers for this last little pup – the runt they called her – what could I do? I couldn't very well leave her, could I?'

'No, you most certainly could not!' answered Molly.

'Not sure it was such a good idea now though,' Albie admitted, wiping his nose on his sleeve. 'Every time I stop the bike to deliver something, she slips her collar and runs into the middle of the road. And the biggest thing is that I have to hide her in the warehouse at night or Dad'll hear her barking and take her down to the RSPCA himself. The poor little thing – she must be terrified in that big, drafty building alone every night. I love her, but it's no life for her. I haven't even given her a name yet – just can't bear to get too attached.'

'Twinkle!' cried Molly.

'What?' Albie and Pippa said together . . . both horrified!

'Her name is Twinkle!' said Molly. 'And she's coming home with us, aren't you, Twinkle?' and she smothered the puppy's head in kisses again.

'Molly, we couldn't possibly. How would we keep her hidden in the dorm . . . where would we get food to feed her? It would never work. And don't even get me started on the name. No self-respecting dog wants to be called *Twinkle*!' Pippa was very nervous about the prospect of taking the puppy back to Garland.

'Don't be such a *worrying-Wilma*, Pippa. Everything you've just said is easily sorted – all except the name change, of course. Didn't you see the twinkle in her eye when she came running up to us? I'm not budging on that. She couldn't possibly be called anything else.'

'Woof!' barked Twinkle on cue, as if in complete agreement with her beautiful new mummy.

Molly looked at Pippa. Pippa looked at Molly. Then both girls looked at Albie.

'Are you sure?' Albie asked, secretly totally relieved to hand over puppy responsibility, after the last twenty-four hours he'd had with her.

'NWCC!' Molly exclaimed. Albie looked at Pippa for a translation.

'No worries chicken curries!' Pippa said, relieved she knew that one.

'Now what else have you got for us in that bike box – or should I say, what's soaking up all the rain from the grass?' Molly asked, oblivious to her Mollyism confusion.

And with that, the deal was done. Pippa was absolutely dreading what Maria would have to say about it, but Molly couldn't have been happier with their new little friend. What fun!

As it happened, Pippa had completely misjudged Maria's reaction. Having managed to smuggle one snuffling, excited puppy and half a dozen Albie parcels past Miss Coates into Garland, Pippa couldn't believe Maria, when they finally reached their room and told her the whole story.

'Told you, Pips,' said Molly with a cheeky grin. 'Mimi only has one weakness in life, which causes her to act with uncharacteristic abandon – animals. Dogs, cats, even mice! I honestly think she'd give her own life before she let someone kill a spider.'

She wasn't wrong, Pippa thought, watching Maria dote on Twinkle.

'Right, Molly. The first thing to accept is that we are going to need help with Twinkle,' Maria said decisively. Molly looked immediately panicked.

'I just mean, we're going to have to get some of the other Garland girls in on this little furry secret of ours. It's going to take too much sneaking about for us three to be able to do it alone.'

'She's right, Molly.' Pippa had now given up worrying and was a fully functioning member of the *Twinkle Rescue Society*. 'Shall I try and catch some of the others now before homework starts? From what I could hear when we came down the corridor earlier, Sally and Belle are definitely back in their rooms.'

'Perfect, Pips. The main thing is that everyone needs to start sneaking food out of the Ivy Room – just until we can get Albie to bring some proper dog food over next week. I just hope Mackle the Jackal isn't back to her itchy, twitchy self today. It's been bliss with her off sick with a bad back these past few weeks. I'd even go so far as to say I've started to enjoy the school food, without her beady eye all over my dining experience.'

Pippa made a face as if she was going to throw up, and ran off to tell the others the exciting news.

'I'm so pleased you agree with me, Mimi. Isn't she just the best, most beautiful dog you've ever seen?'

Twinkle looked up at the twins with huge, brown eyes and, as if she knew making a noise would get her into trouble, she gave the quietest little bark of approval and buried herself under Molly's duvet.

5

Twinkle Twinkle Little Star . . .
How I Wonder Where You Are!

Things with Twinkle went surprisingly smoothly over the next week or so. As you can imagine, the Garland girls, without Lucinda there to upset everyone, had all become very close since returning from the Christmas holidays, and with a secret like Twinkle to knit them together, it was one very happy house.

The only tricky part was taking the puppy for her last toilet trip before lights out. The girls would go in pairs, so that one could keep an eye on Twinkle, and one could keep watch. Only the night before last, Belle and Alice had so nearly been caught by Mr Potts, who was having an evening stroll, that they'd asked the twins for a week off TTD . . .

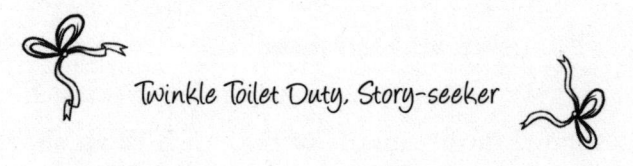

. . . to get their nerve back. The twins and Pippa tended to cover every other evening between them so it wasn't a problem. Tonight however, when it was Molly and Maria's turn on TTD, Molly, Pippa and the rest of Garland it seemed, had got caught up at some after-dinner question and answer session, with a famous British actress, which Maria had no desire to attend. As the clock struck eight-thirty, poor Twinkle was so desperate that Maria decided that just this once, she'd have to take her out alone. Better that than poor Twinkle having an accident. She was such a sensitive little thing. She might never recover from it! Maria grabbed her new fluffy dressing-gown Molly had given her, threw it over them both, and crept into the quad garden, which separated Garland from the main school.

Moments later, a very relieved Twinkle was scurrying around in the bushes while Maria anxiously hid in the shadows. Time's up, Maria thought, but as she called softly to the puppy, she realised she suddenly couldn't hear any dog sounds at all.

'Twin-kle!' she repeated more loudly, venturing

slightly further into the moonlit garden. Suddenly, naughty Twinkle popped her head out from behind the sundial in the middle of the quad. What should Maria do now? The sundial wasn't in the shadows. It was brightly lit, not only by the moon, but also by the lights of the windows on all four sides of the garden. Maria couldn't risk losing her again, so quickly, she ran over to the puppy, and scooped her up under the folds of her dressing-gown.

'So is this the kind of mischief you girls get up to when you think no one's watching?' boomed a deep voice. Both Maria and Twinkle nearly jumped out of their skins, as they swung around to see David Hart, the caretaker, behind them . . .

 . . . and also Miss Hart's father, Story-seeker.

Maria was so shocked that she couldn't think of a single lie to tell. She was also terrified that if she spoke suddenly, the shivering, soggy dog, cosying up for warmth under her dressing-gown, might start barking and give the game away altogether.

'Who does that dog belong to?' Mr Hart asked sternly. Oh no, he's already seen her, Maria realised.

He ignored her silence and continued, 'Don't you

know it's against the school rules to keep pets on the school premises? Hand the dog over immediately – I will have to confiscate it until your parents can come to collect it. And as for your punishment, Miss . . .?' he paused for Maria to give him her name.

'Maria Fitzfoster,' she said, slightly more in control. 'But please Mr Hart . . . please don't phone my parents. You see, the puppy isn't really even mine. We rescued her.'

Mr Hart's expression softened to a look, which Maria knew only too well, as that of a fellow animal lover, the look of unconditional, adoring love for something you've never met before, but just want to help. Twinkle's little black nose was clearly visible now. Defeated, Maria had no choice and held her up to Mr Hart whose heart melted as he smiled at the puppy licking his chin. Maria looked at Twinkle, proudly thinking *clever dog*.

'Miss Fitzfoster, while I appreciate that you seem to have the best of intentions towards this little dog, you will appreciate that now I know of its existence, you can hardly expect me to let you carry on behind the school's back and take it back to your room.'

Maria was beside herself with worry about what Molly and the rest of the girls might say if she came home without Twinkle. At the same time, everything she knew about Miss Hart, and her own instincts, were telling her that Mr Hart was a nice man. She'd already seen from his reaction to Twinkle that he wasn't going to hurt her, so she listened in silence.

'Equally, I think if we go bothering Madame Ruby at this hour, I fear she will have a total melt-down and send me straight to Animal Rescue. So what I suggest is this . . .' he paused. 'I think that I will have to take the puppy home tonight and speak to Helen . . . erm . . . Miss Hart, about what's happened . . .'

Maria's jaw dropped. How could she have got herself into this much trouble so early on in the term – and for doing something so selfless too. Life just wasn't fair.

'Don't worry, Miss Fitzfoster,' Mr Hart said, seeing Maria's expression. 'I'll try and think of something which doesn't give the game away too much about how long you've been hiding this puppy! How long exactly have you been hiding it?' he asked.

'Erm, about two weeks,' Maria answered honestly. It was too late to start making anything up now. 'What will you tell Miss Hart, sir? Please don't say we've been smuggling her into Garland. She'll go crazy at us. We don't have the best track record for not breaking the school rules. But it's always for a good reason, to help someone or other. I'm not sure we wouldn't be expelled for this one. Wouldn't you have done the same when you were our age, sir?' she asked, her big green eyes staring up at him, hopefully.

Mr Hart smiled, trying to remember what it was like to be Maria's age again. 'Yes, I probably would,' he said with a smile. 'Don't worry, I'll think of something which doesn't incriminate you too much when I speak to Miss Hart. I'll say you spotted a stray dog on school property and reported it to me. Then in the morning you can ask Miss Hart's permission to pop into the Support Staff Room to discuss what happens next – whether we advertise in the local community to see whether anyone has lost a puppy, or whether we take it to the local rescue shelter to find a new family, or whether perhaps you would like to speak to your parents about adopting it. Is that a sensible plan, Miss Fitzfoster?' Mr Hart asked, breathing out condensation like a dragon, as he spoke. It really was freezing!

'Oh thank you, Mr Hart. That's so kind of you. Yes please, that would work perfectly. Just one thing though, she didn't come from the local community, so we won't need to do that.'

Mr Hart raised an eyebrow, confused. 'I don't think I want to know any more . . .'

'No, it's nothing bad,' Maria jumped in. 'We didn't steal her or anything. A friend rescued her from certain death, but they couldn't look after her, so we said we would, but if I'm really honest . . . and my sister would kill me for saying this . . . it is all getting a bit too much for us,' she paused for a second. 'Wouldn't you like to keep her yourself, sir? She seems to like you.'

Mr Hart looked down at two more big, beseeching eyes – this time they were brown. 'Well, you are rather adorable aren't you, whatsitsname . . . what is her name anyway?' he asked.

'Twinkle,' Maria said quickly. 'Twinkle, meet Mr Hart, Mr Hart, meet Twinkle. You're going to be the best of friends I can tell!'

'Twinkle?' Mr Hart said. 'Twinkle?' he said again, incredulous at such a silly name. 'Do you think she knows her name yet, or could I change it?'

'Not a chance, sir! She loves it! Thanks so much, . . . see you in the morning, Mr Hart!' Maria cried and ran off back to Garland before he could respond, giggling all the way at the thought of such a big, burly man, calling out to a little dog named *Twinkle*.

Phew, she thought, as she approached their room.

That was a close shave. Thank goodness Mr Hart was a fellow animal lover. She didn't even want to think about what might have happened if he had wanted to report her straight to Miss Hart, or worse, Madame Ruby. Just two more obstacles to overcome, the first to comfort Molly and the rest of the girls for their loss, and the second, to talk Mr Hart into keeping Twinkle. That way everyone won and the girls would get to see her all the time.

Molly woke next morning, red-eyed from a whole night's dramatic grief at losing her little Twinkle.

'I can't bear to see you like this, Moll,' Maria said. 'I promise, promise, promise to convince Mr Hart to keep her and bring her into school. He looked as if he'd like a companion. I just hope Miss Hart believed his story last night.'

'Let's all just focus on how lucky we are that Mr Hart is on our side about this. He could have got us into a world of trouble!' Pippa said, secretly glad not to have to sneak about any more. In fact, all the Garland girls who had been in on Operation Twinkle were sad but relieved someone else was now taking care of the nightly TTD.

'But what if you can't, Mimi – what if she's already on her way to some horrible place with no children and no cuddles?' Molly cried.

'Over my dead body!' Maria answered confidently. 'Look, I'm going to go now to see Miss Hart and ask if she'd mind me speaking to Mr Hart about Twinkle's future . . . I won't tell her we know her name's Twinkle though, obviously! I mustn't forget that we aren't supposed to know her at all. With any luck she'll be impressed that I want to follow up on her welfare.' Maria was interrupted by a note being pushed under the door.

Dear Maria,

My father has brought me up to speed on the events of yesterday evening. What a good eye you must have, spotting a black dog running through the grounds in the pitch-black darkness, from your bedroom window.

'Ha, she's not silly, is she!' Pippa laughed. 'Sorry, carry on . . .'

I am delighted that you followed the correct procedure in reporting the animal's existence, *although it would have been easier for you to tell Miss Coates rather than venturing outside to investigate for yourself. I am only pleased Mr Hart found you when he did.*

Maria winced, but if that was the only telling-off she was going to get, she'd take it!

I understand that you would like to be involved in the decision as to what happens next to the stray, so would you be kind enough to pop over to the Support Staff Room before class to discuss it with Mr Hart at 8:30 a.m. I'm not sure if you've been before – it's located next to Sister Payne's office on the ground floor.

Please ensure that you are not late for your first class of the day.

Regards,

Miss Hart

Maria breathed a sigh of relief.

'Oh that's easy – I'll take you, Mimi. I spent ages there last term after we staged our sprout-choking performance to save Betsy from Mackle the Jackal,' Molly answered.

'Ha!' Pippa exploded, remembering. 'That was so brilliant, you two. I'd forgotten that. I don't think that witch Mackle has ever been able to work out what happened that day.'

'Come on then, Molly – we've only got half an hour if we're going to make it to class for nine. Pips, are you OK to go ahead and cover for us if needs be? We'll try our best to get this sorted out in time though.'

Pippa nodded and the twins disappeared off to meet Mr Hart.

Secretly, Story-seeker, Maria had a few extra topics of conversation for Mr Hart, and hoped half an hour would give them enough time!

★ ★ ★

6

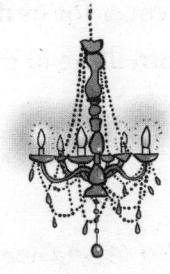

A Very Productive Meeting

*T*he girls heard Twinkle bark as they knocked on the staff-room door, and both immediately felt relieved that she hadn't been given away overnight.

Mr Hart's kind, weathered face appeared at the door; he started as he looked at Maria and then at Molly – the almost identical girls who stood in front of him.

'Twinkle!' Molly exclaimed as the puppy leapt into her arms.

'Sorry, Mr Hart. This is Molly, my twin sister. Hope you don't mind me bringing her along. We've both invested quite a bit of time in Twinkle and Molly's been pretty devastated at the thought of losing her.'

'Of course, it's fine,' Mr Hart answered and signalled to the girls to sit down wherever they could. The office was a bit of a mess with books and paperwork all over the place.

Moments later, Maria had told the whole story of how Twinkle had come to be a refugee at L'Etoile with Molly filling in anything she missed out. Rightly or wrongly, Mr Hart couldn't help but be impressed by the way the girls had rallied round to try and provide a home for her.

'Regardless of any rules that have been broken, what is clear, and I agree with you on this front, is that Twinkle needs a proper place to live, where she isn't permanently at risk of being discovered and sent away. I've no doubt that you and the Garland girls have given her all the love in the world, but a puppy needs freedom to explore and grow into a happy, well-rounded dog. I have to admit, I'd love to give her a home in the caretaker's lodge myself . . .'

Maria, not being one to miss an opportunity, seized her moment. 'Then do it, sir,' she said.

'Yes pleeease, Mr Hart,' Molly said, at which point, Twinkle jumped from her lap to Mr Hart's. She really was a very, very, clever puppy!

'What I mean is . . .' she continued at a pace,

'Twinkle could stay with you. That would work out for everyone, wouldn't it? You get a companion – I can see you love her already, Twinkle gets a wonderful life in the countryside, and the girls and I can see her whenever we like. There isn't really any other option, Mr Hart. I can't bear the thought of her being sent to the rescue home where she'll have to fight for food, fight for a warm place to sleep and, more importantly, fight for a family to notice her and take her home. And who knows what kind of family may come along . . . you never really know what—'

'OK, OK!' David Hart exclaimed. 'I get the picture. But are you sure she doesn't already belong to anyone? Are you really sure?'

'Absolutely positive!' cried Maria, knowing she'd cracked him. 'She's all yours, Mr Hart – aren't you, Twinkle?'

'Woof!' Twinkle barked in agreement.

'Twinkle Hart,' said Molly. 'Has a lovely ring to it, don't you think?'

Maria could have kissed her sister. Molly had no idea that she had just given her the perfect opening for a conversation about the Hart family.

'You're right, Molly – she's definitely a wonderful addition to the Hart family.' She turned to Mr Hart.

'Funnily enough, we've been doing some research on the history of the school and I came across your family tree. You and Miss Hart must be so proud to be related to the great L'Etoile architect, Frank Hart.'

David Hart was completely stunned now. This little girl was so much more mature than her years. It had been a lifetime since he had discussed his ancestry with anyone and it felt good to be asked about the past.

'Why yes, I suppose we are. I thought all that had been long forgotten. My father, Freddie Hart, was also caretaker here at L'Etoile, you know, so you see the Harts have been involved with the school for generations.'

'Did your father ever mention anything to you about *The Legend of the Lost Rose of L'Etoile*?' she asked, innocently.

'Well, now Miss Fitzfoster, how the blazes do you know anything about that? I thought Madame Amber Rose – that was Madame Ruby's mother – had squashed any talk of that, as she didn't want any treasure hunters turning up here, distracting the students from their studies.'

Maria smiled at him. 'Let's just say I can be pretty resourceful when I need to be.'

'Indeed. And it seems I am already a victim of that,' he replied, looking fondly at Twinkle. 'In answer to your question, I know about the legend, of course, but I have absolutely no idea *what* the reported lost treasure is, or *where* it is. My grandfather, Frank, passed away shortly after he is said to have hidden his memorial gift to Lola Rose and, as far as I know, there's no such thing as a treasure map or anything which points to its location.'

'Did Frank leave anything – anything at all – to be passed down through the Hart generations?' Maria pushed, feeling as if she was about at the limit of what she might get away with.

Mr Hart looked thoughtful. 'There is one thing – the only thing, in fact – but it's just an old book about growing roses.'

Maria jumped up, knocking over a tower of books and an empty coffee mug as she did so. 'May we see it?' she asked, scrambling to save the mug before it hit the floor.

'I don't see why not!' he laughed. 'It's somewhere among that lot.' He nodded at the even bigger mess of books and old newspapers strewn all over the floor. Maria turned and caught sight of a large, red leather-bound book sticking out from the pile with the word 'Rose' just visible. She tugged it free.

'*How To Grow The Perfect Rose*,' she read out loud.

Molly had quite forgotten her grief at losing Twinkle as she gleefully watched her sister work her genius.

Trying to maintain a poker face to mask her excitement, Maria said, 'At the risk of pushing our luck, I don't suppose we could borrow this for a couple of days, could we? Might help with a school history project.'

'Be my guest,' said Mr Hart. 'But you won't find anything interesting in there. Just a load of gardening tips – and you don't strike me as particularly green-fingered, Miss Fitzfoster.'

'DING!' The bell sounded to signal the start of school.

'Wow, is it that time already? We'd best get going. Thanks so much for everything, Mr Hart. I know you and Twinkle are going to be very happy together.'

And with that, Maria, followed closely by Molly, planted a huge kiss on the top of Twinkle's head and ran off to class, both confident that there *must* be some kind of clue within the pages of this Hart family heirloom. It just couldn't be a coincidence – *Lola Rose, Legend of the Lost Rose, How To Grow The Perfect Rose*. There simply had to be some meaning hidden within it.

7

How to Grow the Perfect Rose

'*C*lose the door, Moll,' said Maria after they returned from their evening homework session in the library. 'Tonight's the night that we crack this mystery wide open! Pippa, we've got something we need your help with.'

'It's not a kitten, is it?' joked Pippa. 'I'm a bit animal-rescued-out if I'm honest.'

The trio laughed. 'No, Missy P – this has most definitely got nothing to do with the living!' answered clever Maria.

'Grab those chocolate chip cookies and come see,' Molly said, having decided that she could eat junk food, solve a mystery and plait every strand of hair on her head before lights out so she'd have corkscrew curls for the morning.

'Well,' Maria paused. 'There was one more thing to come out of the re-homing Twinkle saga,' she said as she pulled the red, leather-bound book from under her pillow and passed it to Pippa – who thankfully wasn't in hair-braiding mode and had both hands free.

'A book on growing roses?' Pippa asked, confused. 'Great! Like we've got time to start another hobby. Perhaps I'll take up chess too while I'm at it.'

'CO, Pips – it's nothing like that. I thought that at first until I cottoned on to what Maria was thinking,' said Molly.

'OK, OK, I'm *chilling out*. Tell me more,' Pippa answered.

'It's the Hart family heirloom – the only thing to be passed down from generation to generation apparently. I'm convinced it holds a clue to the location of *The Lost Rose of L'Etoile*.'

'Ooooh. Have you found anything?' asked Pippa, turning the pages one by one.

'That's just it, Pips,' said Maria. 'I can't find anything mysterious about it all. I've been looking at it all week now and as far as I can tell, it does exactly what it says on the cover! I can't believe it. I was so sure it was going to be a treasure map of some kind.'

Maria was close to tears. Closer, in fact, than Pippa had ever seen her, and enough to make Molly give up on her braids. She took the book from Pippa.

'And you've been through the whole thing?' she asked.

'Every word – at least five times! I've tried looking for codes within the chapter titles, patterns with the first letter of each line, the last letter of each line, scanning for secret messages, but have come up with precisely nothing!'

Molly turned the pages – starting from the back. 'It even smells old,' she commented, wrinkling her nose and causing Maria to nearly lose her temper, both for stating the obvious, and for reading from back to front!

'And aren't the pages thick? It's like old parchment. It has to be way older than L'Etoile is. There are antique books in the library written around the time L'Etoile was built and even they are not written on paper this thick.'

Pippa felt the pages for herself. 'But wait a minute,' she said quickly. 'You're absolutely right, Molly. These back few pages are much thicker than the ones at the front of the book. Here, Maria, have a feel!'

Maria grabbed the book in astonishment. 'So they are, Pippa, so they are!' she agreed. 'How could I have missed that? I was so obsessed with looking at the words for hidden meanings, I totally didn't notice anything odd about the pages themselves.'

'What if Frank Hart stuck two pages together and the clue is on the inside?' Molly joined in, excited.

'Yes! Well done, girls! That has to be it!' cried Maria. 'An iron, we need an iron!'

'*Fashion Faye Summers*!' they shouted together and Molly ran off to Faye's room to beg, borrow or steal one, if she had to.

'Dah-dah!' she called out, as she arrived back in the doorway, moments later.

'Blimey, that was quick!' said Pippa, plugging it in.

'I know. Luckily, she was on the phone so I didn't get caught up in a conversation.'

By Maria's reckoning, the last six pages were stuck together to make three thick pages. Now that she examined the page numbers more closely, she could see that they had also been tampered with, so that they didn't appear to be incorrectly numbered.

Molly had cleared a space on the end of the bed, and was armed ready with a hot iron and a pillowcase.

'What's the pillowcase for?' asked Pippa.

'We don't want to burn the pages, do we? I say we fold the book open and slide each page into the pillowcase before ironing it – as if we were photocopying it on both sides. The material will soak up some of the steam too and prevent whatever is on the inside from smudging.'

Molly occasionally surprised everyone with her bouts of practicality, Story-seeker.

The girls held their breath as she finished steaming the first page to melt the glue. As she removed the book and picked gently at the corner, the page began to split into two. Amazing! They read what was on the inner pages. Alas, nothing out of the ordinary there, just more tedious rose-growing advice.

'Maybe he had a practice run first?' Pippa suggested. The twins looked blank. 'Quickly, Molly – steam the next one.'

But as she peeled apart the next pair of pages, they were faced with the same, uninteresting print. Maria's face fell. Even Molly looked totally deflated.

'Third time lucky and all that. Don't give up now, Molly,' Pippa said.

As Molly steamed the final pages and stood the

book up to peel them apart, a single sheet of paper fluttered onto the bed.

The girls gasped. Now this was more like it!

As Pippa went to pick it up, Maria grabbed her hand. 'No, Pips. Don't touch it yet. I don't think this piece has anything to do with the rest of the book – which means there's a chance that whatever is on it could be handwritten. Let's let it dry a bit. The steam may have loosened the ink.'

'Good thinking, bat-mite,' agreed Pippa.

With the iron safely switched off, the excited trio stared at the paper on the bed for what seemed like an age.

'Now?' asked Molly desperately. Maria and Pippa both nodded.

As Molly turned the sheet over, they first noticed the crest in the corner with a heart in the centre, and immediately recognised it from the Hart family tree website. It was Frank Hart's family crest.

Remember the crest on the Hart's family tree, Story-seeker?

Maria read the words out loud:

To Whom It May Concern,

If you are reading this, I accept that the time has come for the beauty of my rose to share itself with you and perhaps with the rest of the world. In return, I ask that you make one vow: that, upon discovery of my rose, you do not keep it for yourself, but you ensure that it is returned to the last lady of my line. If you choose to ignore my wishes, you will be cursed to lead a life without love and, believe me, there is no worse punishment.

Yours,

Frank Hart

'W.O.W.,' Molly spelled out.

'Double wow!' said Pippa.

'How cool is that?' said Maria excitedly. 'And there's more. Although goodness only knows what it all means. It's just a load of numbers and symbols.'

The girls looked again at what followed Frank Hart's handwritten note and sat back in dazed confusion.

⇧ ↓ ■ 7 ⇨ □ 4 ⇧ ■ 9 ⇦ ■ 5 ⇧ ■ 2 ⇨ □ ⇧ 🔥 ☉

'I can't possibly take in any more right now. My brain just won't compute a load of gobbledygook like that – not right now anyway,' Pippa said, scratching her head. 'But if I don't try and think about it tonight I'll never get those symbols out of my mind before bed!'

'This just gets more and more unbelievable!' Molly cried as she carefully laid the note back where it had been hiding for over a century. 'Let's talk about it tomorrow. I feel a bit overwhelmed too, if I'm honest.'

Maria laughed, happy in the knowledge that this decoding challenge was right up her street and definitely something she might have some luck with solving alone. She'd already put two and two together and knew that the last lady in Frank's line had to be Miss Hart. So whatever it was he had hidden all those years ago would now belong to her. That should throw the cat among Madame Ruby's pigeons! Now all she had to do was figure out the rest.

8

Back to the Day Job

At the risk of too much talk of adventure, Story-seeker,
we would like you to cast your mind back to the main
focus of the term. Despite our heroines' obsession with
the discovery of the lost rose, we must not forget about
the looming Founder's Day Centenary celebrations.
One must not forget how much preparation a programme
of entertainment worthy of royalty requires!

While Maria's brain worked around the clock
trying to decode Frank Hart's message, the
rest of the school had their knickers in a complete
twist about the forthcoming royal visit.

The first years had asked Miss Hart if they could

take their own music session that afternoon, in order to discuss among themselves which three acts best represented their year group for Madame Ruby's auditions on Friday. Miss Hart was intrigued by the girls' team attitude. Never before had she been faced with such a close-knit year group. Usually there were several fame-hungry students in any year, ready and willing to trample on another girl to get to the top. It seemed that ever since Lucinda Marciano had decided not to return for the spring term, the first-year girls had united in their delight. Miss Hart thought what a lovely change it made, and she was happy to grant their wish.

'Right then, we've only got an hour to come up with something that will knock the other years out of the park!' exclaimed singer, Alice.

'Why don't we start by writing a list of everyone who thinks they've prepared something really special – then we'll know what we've got to choose from,' suggested the dancer, Elizabeth Jinks.

'Good idea, Jinksie,' ballet dancer Heavenly answered. 'Bags do the writing,' she continued, as she pirouetted over to the whiteboard at the front of Mozart Room 1.

'Great. Who's up first?' Elizabeth asked, looking

round the room. 'OK, I'll start us off shall I? Amanda, Heavenly and I have been working on this *Swan Lake* ballet routine since we got back. Can't get it out of my head since I saw it on Christmas Eve. We're pretty pleased with ourselves and it's just about ready, so we'd like to throw that into the mix if that's all right with the rest of you?'

'Ooooh, that sounds lovely,' said Faye. 'I can see the beautiful costumes now – we'd need a lorry-load of feathers from somewhere, though.'

Charlotte and Sofia nudged each other and both put their hands up. 'Not sure if it's what you're looking for,' Charlotte addressed the group, 'but Sofia and I have been trying to write our own opera number. We've got the melody and lyrics – we're just not convinced it sounds right sung in English.'

'Exactly!' Sofia joined her. 'I'm waiting for my father to email me the correct Italian translation so that we can try that. I think it'll be a million times better, to be honest. Everything sounds so much more dreamy in Italian.'

'Sounds lovely!' Pippa said. 'That's definitely in the mix. How clever of you both.'

Molly, who had been going out of her mind trying to think of something she'd performed before, was suddenly struck with a brainwave. 'Talking of clever, Pippa, I've just had the best idea!'

'What?' said at least ten of the girls, in unison.

'Well,' started Molly, 'when we came back after Christmas, Pippa played us a song she's written about friendship. It's fantastic! It's current, punchy, great lyrics, and has a wicked beat too.'

Pippa blushed crimson.

'What I was thinking was, that we're at our best when we come together as a group and combine all our talents. What if we only submit one piece – an orchestral/choral version of Pippa's song? It would be so strong and I bet no one's ever done it before.'

'Brilliant!' cried Sally. 'I haven't even heard it and I love it already. Beats performing a solo any day! Don't think I'm ready for that again just yet.'

Molly looked around the room to check that everyone was happy. The girls' reaction was even better than she'd hoped for. Everyone was beaming. The atmosphere had turned from glum to glee in one hit. Molly loved it when a plan came together!

'Why don't you go and get the track, Pippa, so we can get cracking. I can't wait to hear it,' said Daisy. 'What a brilliant idea!'

While Pippa scooted back to Garland to collect

her iPod, cellist Lydia started to work out whether they had a full house of instruments and players between them for the orchestra. They'd have Maria, Autumn and Betsy on keys; herself on strings, Daisy on woodwind, Lara on percussion. That left a choir of eleven: the singers, Pippa, Molly, Sofia, Charlotte, Corine and Alice – plus the dancers, Amanda, Belle and Heavenly, who all had beautiful voices too. The actresses Sally and Nancy would also join the choir and of course there'd be Faye on wardrobe! It just might work, Lydia thought excitedly.

As Pippa docked her iPod and played her song 'Friends Forever', the girls fell silent. By the first chorus, every single head in the room was bobbing to the beat and Belle was twirling around.

'What do you think?' asked Pippa, terrified, when the track ended.

'BRILLIANT!!' the girls shouted back. 'Marvellous ... you're so clever ... what a song!'

Pippa glowed with pride. 'Well, if you're all sure?'

'Sure?' cried Alice. 'It'll blow their socks off!'

'Pippa, I think you and Molly should take this idea to Miss Hart after class,' Lydia said. 'Tell her it's what we've all decided we really want to do, in a we-won't-take-no-for-an-answer kind of way.'

'Sure thing, jelly bean,' Molly said. 'I'm so pleased you're all on board with this idea. A good afternoon's work, girls. Pippa – will you start working with Maria, Lydia and the girls on the musical parts, and I'll figure out some harmonies with the singers. Then I think we should get together again on Thursday afternoon for a proper full group rehearsal so we're ready to perform it to Madame Ruby in the auditions on Friday.'

'Blimey, we've left ourselves quite a challenge time-wise,' Pippa said, feeling worried.

'This isn't a challenge, Pips. You know all about a challenge!' Molly whispered, reminding her about Frank Hart's coded message. She turned to the group. 'I'll burn off a load of CDs with the track on and bring them to supper, so you can each have a copy. Let's give old Mackle something else to moan about!'

The group went back to their rooms, feeling excited and proud about their decision to enter as one act. They just hoped Miss Hart and Madame Ruby would agree with them!

9

A Revealing Rehearsal

The meeting with Miss Hart went very well indeed. She seemed overjoyed that the first years had been so generous to one another, having found a way that they could all shine in a single performance. Molly and Pippa left her on the phone to Madame Ruby explaining why there would only be one first-year act performing for her on Friday.

'Rather her than me!' giggled Molly, scrabbling about in her bag for her new *Glimmerglass* lipgloss.

'Ha! I know. Knowing what we do now about Miss Hart always having lived in Madame Ruby's shadow at the school, I admire her being brave enough to try new things,' Pippa said.

After supper, the whole year took their CDs back to their dorms to listen and learn every note and lyric of 'Friends Forever' so that they'd be ready for the next day's rehearsal. Unfortunately, the Mozart Music Rooms and the Kodak Hall had already been booked by other year groups, but Miss Hart had come up with the idea of using the main L'Etoile entrance hall. It was big enough to accommodate them all – and in actual fact, if the choir stood on the steps of the grand spiral staircase with the mini-orchestra below, they'd all be able to see their conductor – which, of course, would be the lovely Pippa.

'I just don't know how I'm going to write up all the parts for the orchestra in time for tomorrow,' Pippa said, as she got into bed with a pencil and a wadge of music paper.

'I just might be the answer to all your problems!' said Maria, looking up from her laptop. 'I figured we'd be under pressure, and I've had a reply from Miss Hart agreeing to excuse us both from tomorrow morning's lessons.'

'You're joking!' Pippa exclaimed, a look of pure relief crossing her face. 'Oh, Maria, I don't know why I don't think of these things. That makes the world of difference. Thank you sooooooo much!'

'Listen, you're the artist! I'm the practical one. Together, we're dynamite!' Maria answered.

'What am I? Pedigree Chum?' said Molly, hurt at being left out.

'You, sister dear, are the icing on the cake of our little operation,' Maria answered. 'Where would we be without your belief and your beauty – not to mention your harmonies in that choir tomorrow?'

Molly smiled and the happy trio sat up working on their parts for 'Friends Forever' until the early hours.

♡

'I truly think that this might be my favourite room at L'Etoile,' Molly exclaimed, as she helped Maria fix up the keyboard in the entrance hall.

'Just look at that sweeping staircase . . . and that big old fireplace . . . and wasn't Lola Rose beautiful,' she continued, gazing up at the portrait that hung above the fireplace. The artist had captured Lola Rose's face so perfectly. Her skin was like porcelain, warmed by the glow of the fire below. And her eyes seemed to watch over the entire room, taking in every student, teacher and guest who passed through the L'Etoile doors.

All at once, the rest of the first years filed in noisily from various different directions.

Pippa was setting up a music stand in the centre of the hall, to ensure she was perfectly positioned for both the choir snaking round the staircase, and the mini-orchestra below. Maria began handing out scores to the musicians, sincerely hoping the girls could read her and Pippa's rushed efforts.

'What, you've written all these parts since yesterday?' Betsy said, looking impressed.

'Yep! Maria and I have been up all night!' said Pippa, whose wild raven hair was even more crazy as a result.

'The only part we couldn't do, Lara, is your drums. We figured you're the best person to work that bit out,' said Maria, somewhat hopefully.

'I've already nailed it!' answered Lara, triumphantly. 'I set my alarm for five o'clock this morning, so I could get into one of the Mozart percussion rooms before they were booked. Can you believe it – the third years had filled every available rehearsal space by seven o'clock. What a bunch of saddos!'

'You won't be saying that if their contribution puts ours to shame tomorrow,' muttered Daisy, as she looked through a very complicated woodwind part, which meant her changing from the bassoon to the clarinet, and back again, halfway through the song.

'Daisy, chill out. You'll breeze through this!' said Pippa, giving her arm an affectionate squeeze. 'Do you think Maria would have written you something you couldn't do with your eyes shut?' Daisy blushed and started to practise.

Molly had arranged the singers on the stairs – tallest (Alice) at the bottom, to shortest (Belle) at the top, so that they looked more on one level.

This had given Faye the chance to see them all together and think what might work best for costumes. Should they go for a classical choir-type uniform, which would clash with the modern song they were singing? Or should they go as themselves, but with some sort of theme attached? Yes, that was it. They'd go in their own clothes, to be as up-to-date as Pippa's song, but dress head-to-toe in white – to make them look like angels on this special occasion.

'I don't know why it matters where we stand today, Moll,' said the pianist, Autumn, as Molly moved her around in the choir line for the third time. Autumn had decided to join the choir, as Maria and Betsy had the piano parts covered. Singing would make a lovely change for her. 'We'll be performing on one level on the Kodak stage for the real thing.'

'I know, I know. I just think we'll rehearse better if

we look good,' Molly answered, feeling a bit silly.

'Erm, Molly, I see what you're trying to do,' Heavenly added, 'but surely we should be standing in our vocal groups – say, altos at the bottom, and sopranos at the top?'

'Oh my goodness, how stupid do I feel now!' cried Molly. She couldn't believe she'd forgotten that bit. Well, this was her first choir. 'OK girls – just stand in your vocal groups like we did last night.'

'Right everyone,' Pippa suddenly announced. 'How do you feel about doing a quick run-through of the whole song – just to see what we're dealing with here?'

'Yep . . . yes . . . sure . . . ready . . .' came a multitude of replies.

As Pippa raised her conductor's baton – or in this case, one of Faye's knitting needles – to signify the start, Lara brought the beat down on one of two drums she was improvising with, not having been able to bring a full kit.

The singers sang their hearts out – filling the entrance hall with their beautiful, flawless harmonies. And the orchestra managed to muddle through the song, most of the girls sight-reading their parts for the first time.

By the time Pippa brought the needle down for the last beat, she and at least half a dozen other girls were shaking with excitement.

'Blimey, we're a bit good, ain't we!' Alice Parry summed it up in the only way she could.

Faye, the only spectator, was jumping up and down on the big leather armchair by the front door, whooping. 'Girls, that was flippin' amazing!' she cried, confirming what they all felt.

Maria tried to put on her best serious face. 'Calm down, girls; after all, we're a whole afternoon's worth of rehearsals away from feeling one hundred per cent about this performance – but I will say this,' and her face cracked into the biggest, cheekiest grin she could muster, 'Good luck to the rest of the school – they're gonna need it!'

Everyone exploded into claps and cheers and the rehearsals continued until the bell sounded for supper.

'Can you believe how well this afternoon went, Mimi?' Molly asked as she collected the rest of the lyric sheets. 'Everyone's worked so well together to make this happen. Pippa must be delighted with the result.'

'Yes, it's going to be fantastic. I can't wait for

Miss Hart to see it tomorrow. I reckon she'll be the proudest person in the room.' Maria paused for a moment, watching her crazy sister scurry around like a lunatic, picking things up and dropping them at the same time.

'Molly, how is it that, for someone so immaculately presented, you really are the most disorganised person at L'Etoile? Hurry up, will you – the others left ages ago and I'm starving!'

'Hang on . . . two more seconds. OK, I'm done. I just want to make sure we've left everything exactly as we found it. You might call it being slow, I call it being thorough!' Molly answered. 'If you're in that much of a hurry, why don't we go out of the front door and run round the outside to the Ivy Room. It'll be so much quicker than going through the school.'

'Good thinking,' said Maria as she unlatched the huge double doors to L'Etoile.

Just a couple of footsteps behind Maria, Molly managed to trip over the doormat, falling with a thud – closely followed by her satchel, spilling papers and various make-up brushes all over the steps.

Maria turned in alarm to see her twin lying spread-eagled, halfway out of the entrance to their grand school. Thank goodness they were alone, she thought.

'Moll,' she cried out in alarm. 'Are you all right?'

Molly started to giggle. 'I'm fine . . . it's just my ego that's bruised. Don't worry, Mimi, you're unbearable when you're hungry. You go on and I'll catch you up.'

Maria couldn't help feeling irritated by Molly's clumsiness on this occasion, and felt an eye-rolling moment was appropriate. As she raised her eyes, she noticed the huge gold L'Etoile star door knocker, glinting in the light directly above where Molly was scrabbling around. All at once, something in her mind clicked and she was reminded of Frank Hart's letter. She whipped it out from her sleeve – which was where she'd decided was the safest place to hide it. She looked again at the symbols and then up at the star. A huge, smug grin spread across her face. Thank goodness for clumsy, clever, Molly, she thought and ran off to supper.

But, Story-seeker, further investigations would have to wait.

10

One Step Closer

*M*aria decided not to distract the others with her latest discovery – not until she was absolutely sure her suspicions were correct. She decided to wait until the Friday audition performance to Madame Ruby was out of the way. Everyone was in such a panic about it, despite how wonderfully the rehearsal had gone.

As the first years sat in The Kodak Hall watching the other year groups' entries, they felt sick with nerves.

'Imagine what we're going to be like next Friday when we do this for real in front of the prince!' whispered Betsy.

'Oh, don't even say the "P" word,' groaned Lara. 'I've no idea how I'm going to keep the drum beat straight when my heart is pounding to a different one in my chest!'

Pippa was quietly taking it all in, watching the audition pieces from other year groups. She felt so proud that her friends had chosen her song as their only entry. It was at that moment that she suddenly realised she'd never felt this complete before. As an only child, she'd never known what it felt like to have such closeness with people her own age. She was, of course, immensely close to her mother and Uncle Harry, but having all these wonderful girls around her made her feel special in a different way – a way that made her want to do anything for them.

'Earth to Pippa Burrows,' said Molly.

'Eh? Sorry? Oh, Molly, I was miles away,' Pippa answered.

'I could see that, Pips. Is everything all right?' Molly asked, always concerned when anyone fell silent for more than two seconds.

'Couldn't be better!' exclaimed Pippa, giving her best friend an unexpected hug.

'And now, L'Etoilettes,' Madame Ruby's voice sounded through the speaker system. 'To our last audition piece. Can we have the one and only first-year entry . . . I must say, girls, it's quite a risk you've taken, putting all your eggs in one basket like this. I just hope it's good enough.'

'Come on, girls. Let's get this show on the road!' said Lydia, ponytail swinging as she led the way.

The first years ran over to the stage and got themselves ready. As Pippa stepped onto the conductor's podium and raised her knitting needle, she gave the group a huge grin, which they immediately returned and began to play and sing their hearts out.

Even before Maria had finished playing the last few notes, the Kodak Hall audience, including Miss Hart, were on their feet applauding. Molly was sure she'd even seen Madame Ruby make a move to stand up at one point, before she checked herself and resumed her usual poker-faced expression.

'Thank you, first years,' said Miss Hart as she collected the microphone. 'I know Madame Ruby would agree that that was a truly inspiring and cutting-edge performance, girls.'

The whole room looked immediately to Madame Ruby for her reaction. After an agonising pause, she gave the slightest nod of approval, but that was enough for a few squeals of delight from the likes of Betsy and Belle.

Madame Ruby's only addition to Miss Hart's commentary was, 'I would like to make one request – that Miss Burrows exchanges that ridiculous knitting needle for a proper conductor's baton from Mr Potts at her earliest convenience. It wouldn't do for us to be seen without the correct equipment now, would it?'

Maria could have screamed. That old bat! She just couldn't let the performance go without throwing in a negative, could she!

Miss Hart took to the microphone again. 'Thank you for all of your efforts. The final running order for the show will go up on the board outside the Ivy Room by the time you've finished supper this evening, so that you can all enjoy your weekend. You are now dismissed, girls.'

'To us!' said Pippa, standing and raising her glass of water to all the first-year girls at supper. 'We totally rock!'

'Cheers!' they all shouted back, clinking glasses and slopping water everywhere.

'Wait until you're all wearing white for the real

thing next week,' Faye said. 'It'll push the whole performance up another notch – if that's even possible. Well done, everyone. You really did leave the rest of the school standing. There wasn't anything new or exciting about any of their performances. I can see why they all played it so safe and chose classical pieces, but could they have been any more yawn-boring?'

'Thanks, Faye!' said Autumn. 'Now that's what I call a critique. Next time, why don't you do the feedback for Madame Ruby?' The girls all fell into a fit of giggles.

'GIRLS! WE'RE IN!' Charlotte and Sofia shrieked, as they came hurtling through the Ivy Room towards their classmates.

'Oh thank goodness!' cried Pippa.

'Yes, and that's not all, we're going to close the show!' Sofia explained. 'We're late as we got caught up helping Mr Potts tidy, but as a result we made it here just in time to see Miss Hart pinning the running order up outside the Ivy Room. Can you believe it? We – the first years – are the headline act! Isn't that just amazing?'

Pippa thought she might burst with happiness.

The celebrations continued until lights out. None of the girls could believe they'd beaten off competition from the senior years to get the top slot in the Founder's

Day Centenary entertainment programme. What an honour! As an extra special sneaky treat, Pippa had spread the word among their year that there would be a secret jelly-sweet midnight feast in their room, at the slightly earlier time of ten-thirty. No one would be able to stay up as late as midnight for gossip and wine gums after the euphoric day they'd had.

'You two still awake?' Maria asked Molly and Pippa when everyone had left. 'Can you believe the Monroe girls had the guts to sneak over to us tonight. It's so cool!'

'I know Pips. WATC.' said Molly.

What are the chances, Story-seeker!
Do let us know when you no longer need
Mollyism translations won't you?

'Totes well done for organising – it was an inspired idea. No idea how we managed to fit everyone in here though. It looks like a bomb has gone off. I swear there are strawberry shoelaces stuck in between the floorboards!' Pippa giggled.

'I might have something else a little inspiring for you too,' said Maria suddenly.

'Ooooh I just love a Maria late-night revelation!'

whispered Pippa excitedly, grabbing her new 'Pippa' white fluffy dressing-gown from the back of the bedroom door. 'Do tell!'

'You know our little treasure hunt? Let's just say I might have had a bit of a breakthrough with decoding Frank's message,' Maria answered triumphantly.

'How can you possibly have had time to think about that these past couple of days, with everything else that's been going on?' asked Pippa, aware that Maria had been dutifully at her side helping with the musical arrangements, ever since they'd made the decision to perform her song.

Maria smiled. 'It was thanks to Molly really,' she said.

'What?' Molly asked, confused. 'What did I do?'

Maria explained how Molly's clumsy fall after their rehearsal the other night, had led to her noticing the big gold L'Etoile star door knocker, which had in turn, reminded her of the first symbol:

⇧

'I'm ninety-nine per cent sure that the first arrow pointing up, followed by a star, is our starting point to crack this mystery. We need to get back into the entrance hall with the code, and look for other things there that might relate to the symbols.'

Pippa and Molly were shocked at Maria's discovery. She was a genius even when she wasn't trying to be!

'I keep trying to picture the hall, but just can't in enough detail to solve this without physically being there. And now that whole area is annoyingly out of bounds while the security teams move in to prepare for the royal visit . . .' Maria went on.

'Oh no!' exclaimed Molly. 'Do you mean we're going to have to wait until after Founder's Day before we can get in to have a proper look? Knowing what we know now, I don't think I can bear it.'

'My sentiments exactly,' Maria whispered. 'I've been looking online for any photos of the entrance hall, to see if we can work through the line of code but, would you believe, there isn't a single shot anywhere of the whole room. There are lots of close-ups of Lola Rose's portrait and the staircase – even the black entrance doors, with the star knocker – but not as a complete room.'

'I don't know what to say. Could this be any more frustrating?' said Pippa, exasperated.

'I know!' Molly said suddenly. 'What about asking Mr Hart if he's got any old pictures lying around?

Surely the Hart family have taken loads of pictures of the school over the years.'

'Of course!' Maria cried. 'Why didn't I think of that? I'm so stupid!'

'Don't be daft,' Pippa said. 'Sometimes you just need a fresh mind on a situation – even you, brain-box!'

'Oh girls, what would I do without you?' Maria exclaimed, as she jumped out of bed to give them both a hug.

'That's settled, then. I'm bound to see Mr Hart working in the gardens in the morning. I can ask him about it.'

'We'll come too,' said Molly. 'I'm desperate for cuddles with Twinkle-pooch!'

'What, are my cuddles not good enough for you any more, Moll?' Maria joked.

At that, Pippa launched a well-aimed pillow at the pair of them and flicked the lamp off.

11

A Weekend of Disappointment

'Where can he and Twinkle have gone to? Mr Hart never leaves L'Etoile!' Maria groaned, when there was no sign of him working anywhere in the grounds.

'I hope it's not something serious,' Molly answered. 'Don't forget, it is Saturday. Generally, people have stuff to do on Saturday.'

'Yes, me! I have something of the utmost importance to do today,' Maria said, jumping up and down on the spot.

'Calm down, Maria,' said Pippa. 'Look, let's come back later. The bus leaves to take us swimming in half an hour anyway. Mr Hart will probably be home by the time we get back. Let's try and forget about this for a couple of hours.'

But much to the girls' annoyance, Mr Hart didn't come back that evening. And he still wasn't home on Sunday afternoon.

'I just can't believe our luck,' said Maria. 'Usually I see that man pottering about the school seven days a week, fixing something or other. Isn't it just typical that the one time we actually need him, he's decided to do a disappearing act!'

'Why don't you write him a note saying you were hoping to catch him to see if he has any old photos of the school for your history project, and pop it through the lodge front door. That way you'll be sure to get his attention as soon as he's back, and he might have a look straight away,' Pippa suggested.

'Pippa's right, Mimi. Do it now, so we can go down and watch the Sunday night movie with the others. It'll do us all good to switch off for a bit. All we've done is rehearse and look for Mr Hart and Twinkle this weekend. I'm pooped!'

'All right,' Maria said, beaten. 'I'll do it now.' And no sooner had she sat down to write to Mr Hart with her request for photos, than she was out of the door, posting the envelope through the letterbox before hot-footing it back to the TV room to join the others.

Maria was absolutely exhausted as she filed out of assembly on Monday morning. It seemed that having a little knowledge about something but not being able to do anything with it was far worse than having no knowledge at all. Her imagination had kept her awake half the night – to the point where she couldn't remember which of her theories about the Lost Rose was based on reality and which she'd dreamed up. And to top it off, Madame Ruby had announced that everyone was to follow her to the lake straight after assembly, for some boring Founder's Day tree-planting ceremony, so she'd have to wait even longer!

'Come on, Mimi!' Molly said, linking her sister's arm. 'You're really not with it today, are you? Mr Hart will come and find you soon – I'm sure of it!'

Maria grunted back at her as they reached the clearing, named Founder's Copse, on the other side of the lake. Madame Ruby stood in the centre, sporting black wellington boots and armed with an enormous spade. At her feet was a pre-dug hole, with a young silver birch tree standing in it, and an enormous pile of earth, ready to be scooped and scattered onto the tree's roots.

'L'Etoilettes,' she said, 'it is with an enormous amount of pleasure that I give root to this silver birch, to commemorate one hundred years of our beloved L'Etoile. May it grow in strength like the ninety-nine other Founder's Day ceremony trees you see around you, and encourage the same growth in the success of L'Etoile for many more centuries to come.'

As the audience of staff and students clapped and watched, she moved a tiny pile of soil into the hole and then laid the spade back down on the ground.

'Is that it?' Alice whispered to the twins. She'd been looking forward to seeing Madame Ruby break a sweat, filling that big hole up with earth.

'I'm amazed she managed to lift one shovelful,' Molly giggled, 'with those matchstick arms. I reckon even Betsy's got more muscles!'

'I heard that, Moll,' Betsy whispered. 'But you're absolutely right. I reckon I'd beat old Ruby in an arm wrestle any day.'

The girls doubled up laughing. The mental image of Madame Ruby, sitting with her sleeves rolled up, face to face with little Betsy, was too funny for words.

Maria however, was, as usual, distracted by her own thoughts. As soon as they'd arrived at the lake and she'd seen the immaculate tree-planting preparations, she knew Mr Hart must be back. Who else could have set up the tree-planting ceremony so beautifully?

Suddenly, almost magically, Maria spotted Twinkle bounding through the trees around the circle of onlookers. Amazingly, no one else had seemed to notice her yet. And what was that she was carrying in her mouth?

By the time she had reached Maria, some of the other girls had spied her and were pointing and calling out. Molly, who had also just spotted her, was patting her thighs and calling, 'Come on Twinkle, here girl,' over and over again.

Twinkle, however, was a puppy on a mission and dutifully ignored everyone, including Molly! Instead, she stopped right in front of Maria, dropped a small cellophane-wrapped envelope at Maria's feet, gave a quick bark to say 'There you go, Little Miss Impatient,' and scampered back off into the bushes, as though she'd never been there.

Maria, seeing a furious-looking Miss Hart making a beeline for them, quickly stuffed the puppy-slobbered envelope under her jumper, hoping no one had noticed it, and tried to appear as confused as the rest of the girls by what had just taken place.

'Girls, was that a dog I just saw running loose around the copse?' Miss Hart asked, expectantly. 'Thank goodness Madame Ruby didn't witness that. She'd have had a heart attack.'

'Erm, Miss Hart,' Pippa said quietly. 'I think it was actually Mr Hart's new puppy, Twinkle.'

Miss Hart suddenly went very red, having quite forgotten about her father's newly acquired pet.

'Well, if you see her again, would you kindly come and find me or Mr Hart and return her? I don't want to think what will happen if she runs amok in Madame Ruby's precious rose garden!'

'We will, Miss, don't worry,' said Molly. 'Although I'm sure she's back in her bed as we speak.'

Miss Hart raised an eyebrow. There was something else afoot here. These ladies seemed just too sure of their answers about something they shouldn't really know anything about. She must remember to pay her father a visit later to see what he had to say for himself and the puppy!

'OK, ladies. Thank you for your . . . your . . . input. Off to class with you now. We all have a very big day ahead of us tomorrow. After all, it's not every day you meet a member of the Royal Family is it?'

The girls nodded and ran off to what was left of their history lesson, desperate to sneak a peek at whatever was in Twinkle's surprise delivery!

12

Founder's Eve

Maria took a detour via the Ladies on her way to history class. She couldn't wait a second longer to see if there was anything useful in Twinkle's envelope.

Even before she'd slammed the cubicle door shut and flipped down the loo seat, she'd torn the envelope open.

> *Dear Maria,*
>
> *I'm very sorry to have missed you this weekend. Twinkle and I took a wonderful trip up to the Lake District to a special forestry estate to collect Madame Ruby's silver birch, ahead of this morning's centenary planting ceremony. Madame is very specific, as you well know, but we didn't mind, as it gave Twinkle an opportunity to chase rabbits*

for a whole day!

I've had a good hunt around for any old pics of L'Etoile but, to be honest, there aren't all that many. Have you tried the Founder's book in the library? Of course you will have, silly question. Anyway, I've enclosed what I have – hope Twinkle hasn't dribbled over everything!

Keep them safe for me and I'll collect them from you when all of this royal visit madness is over.

Best wishes,

David Hart

Ps. Twinkle misses you girls!

Maria's first thought, as she opened the envelope within the envelope, was how uncannily like his grandfather's Mr Hart's handwriting was. She held her breath as she pulled out several photographs of the school. The first three were incredibly old, brown and white sepia shots of the Kodak Hall and the Mozart Rooms while they were being built. The fourth was a picture of a handsome man standing at the entrance to L'Etoile. Frank Hart, Maria whispered to herself, feeling as though this dream world where she'd tried to imagine Frank's final days, searching for a place to hide his treasure, had finally come to life. The last picture would, to most people, have appeared to be the least interesting, showing the chessboard-type black and white floor tiles being laid in the entrance hall. But to Maria, this was the jackpot! As she stared at the photograph, and then back at Frank's coded message, which she'd laid on her lap, it was as though the symbols were all jumping out at her, revealing their secret meaning.

⇪ ⬇ ■ 7 ⇨ ☐ 4 ⇪ ■ 9 ⇦ ■ 5 ⇪ ■ 2 ⇨ ☐ ⇪ 🔥 ☉

Using a mixture of her memory of the room, the photograph of the floor and a little bit of her genius, Maria smiled the biggest smile you've ever seen. She, Maria Fitzfoster, in that moment, was pretty convinced she had solved *The Legend of the Lost Rose*. And tomorrow night, under the cover of darkness, she would take the girls on a real-life treasure hunt!

'Mimi – we totally lost you! I bet you sneaked off to take a look at what Mr Hart sent for us,' Molly said as Maria sat down at the desk next to her.

Maria grinned at her sister. She could never tell her a lie, but equally, there was absolutely nothing they could do about the *Lost Rose* until Founder's Day was over and all the extra bodies had gone back to London.

So Maria decided that she would keep quiet and hope the others would be too wrapped up in the imminent arrival of *Prince Charming* to notice.

'Nothing much, Moll. No obvious "X" marks the spot or anything. But never mind that now. What have I missed? Can't believe I've managed to make it here before old Butter-boots! And I thought I was late.'

'No, she was here, but she's popped out to collect some print-outs of the Founder's Day running order for us. At last I think we might be about to find out what exactly is happening tomorrow. With any luck, they might even spill the beans on our royal visitor.'

The noise level in the history room was deafening, due to the excited chatter of half a dozen very giddy girls. In fact, there wasn't a soul at L'Etoile, students, teachers or facilities staff, who wouldn't have been lying if they said they weren't just a teeny bit excited about tomorrow.

'Here you are, girls,' announced Mrs Butter as she returned to the classroom, her arms flailing with a wadge of schedules. 'Lara, dear, would you do the honours? I'm quite breathless from running up to the staff room and back. I really must remember to go back to my aerobics class,' she muttered.

As Lara handed the sheets out, Pippa began to read out loud:

ONE HUNDRED YEARS OF L'ETOILE, SCHOOL FOR THE PERFORMING ARTS

* * *

9 a.m.–12 p.m. Final dress rehearsal for performances in the Kodak Hall with Miss Hart

12:30 p.m. Hot buffet lunch in the Founder's Day marquee to the rear of the Ivy Room

1:30 p.m. Seats to be taken in the Kodak Hall

2 p.m. A royal arrival marks the start of the Founder's Day ceremony

2:05 p.m. Special Founder's Day speech by Emmett Fuller, President, Universal Music

2:20 p.m. Special awards ceremony presented by HRH TBC

2:45 p.m. Special student entertainment performances:

YEAR 6 - Orchestral Arrangement of 'Clair de lune'

YEAR 5 - A Soprano Trio

YEAR 3 - A Percussion Extravaganza

YEAR 2 - A Modern Twist on a Shakespeare Classic

YEAR 4 - A Royal Dance Medley

YEAR 1 - The First-Year Choir and Orchestra Perform 'Friends Forever'

3:30 p.m. A royal send-off - students and staff to line the drive and wave off HRH TBC

4 p.m. Memory box contributions with form tutors

7 p.m. Fireworks by the lake (weather permitting)

'HRH! HIS ROYAL HIGHNESS!!!' Molly squealed with delight. 'They've slipped up there, girls. It's just got to be Prince Henry. It's got to! Oh but what can I do with my hair . . . it's got to be something he'll never have seen before!'

Maria couldn't bring herself to burst Molly's bubble and say that HRH could also mean *Her* Royal Highness.

'I hope so. I'm keeping my fingers crossed, my toes crossed and my eyes crossed!' Alice joked. 'My dad nearly fainted when I told him a prince might be paying me a visit this week!'

'And I see Mr Fuller's coming too,' Pippa said, feeling more proud than ever now that he would see the girls performing one of her songs. 'This whole thing just couldn't have worked out any better.'

'I think he's kind of handsome for an older chap,' Sofia commented, having also met Mr Fuller after the Christmas gala.

'So does Miss Hart!' giggled Maria.

'Maria! You can't say that!' Molly snapped. 'You'd be hit with the biggest legal case for slander if you were a real journalist. You have to have proof of the facts before you start spreading gossip like that.'

'Oh Molly, it's just a bit of harmless fun,' Maria

insisted. 'Anyway, you saw the way those two looked at each other at Christmas. Can you honestly say, in your heart of hearts, there's nothing going on there?'

'Really? How lovely!' Sofia said dreamily. All the girls loved Miss Hart. And it was nice for them to think of her happy and in love with such a successful man – if it was true, of course.

'Well, I just don't think we ought to be spreading rumours at the moment. Don't want to jinx it for them, do we?'

The truth is, Story-seeker, that Emmett Fuller and Helen Hart were hopelessly in love. They'd met many years ago, when Miss Hart was in her twenties, trying to make it as a singer, and Mr Fuller was a young record company talent scout. He had been besotted with her since the first time he'd heard her sing. Miss Hart had had such a promising career as a singer with Mr Fuller behind her, but when Madame Ruby's mother – Amber Rose D'Arcy, the headmistress of L'Etoile, the lady who had treated Miss Hart like a daughter, giving her all the opportunities she afforded her own daughter – fell desperately ill, Miss Hart gave up her dreams of stardom, to nurse Amber Rose until she died some years later. It is indeed a tragic tale of sacrifice, Story-seeker, but one that must be told if you are to understand the love and attraction between two people whose circumstances kept them apart when they were young, and then reunited them later in life in love. The Christmas gala was the first time Miss Hart and Mr Fuller had seen each other in over a decade. And they'd barely been out of each other's company and thoughts since.

'I'll soon let you know if there's anything magical going on between them,' Belle joined in. 'I'm a bit witchy about these sorts of things. I can always tell, you know.'

'Don't be daft, Belle Brown!' Amanda said. 'Next you'll be telling me Mr Potts is about to propose to old Butter-boots!'

The girls fell about laughing.

13

The Big Day Arrives

'I officially hate anyone who managed to get a good night's sleep last night,' Molly groaned, as she saw how dull her tired eyes looked in the mirror. 'Honestly, it was as if everyone was up, pacing corridors and clunking about. They should have called this place L'Etoile, School for Over-Excited Insomniacs!'

'Nothing a bit of expertly-applied make-up can't fix, I hope,' Pippa mumbled, feeling exactly the same way, as she climbed out of bed. 'Do you think it's like this the night before your wedding day?'

'Goodness, I hope not. I couldn't bear that. Remind me of this, will you, when the time comes? I'll need to hire a hypnotist or something to send me off to sleep,' Molly replied.

'Are you two girls seriously having this conversation?' Maria looked up, laughing at her daft room-mates. 'Here, what do you think of this? Just read the last bit before I upload it,' she said, reading out her Founder's Day *Yours, L'Etoilette* blog.

TO BE OR NOT TO BE: A RIGHT ROYAL SUCCESS?

. . . and so, L'Etoilettes, we go once more into the Kodak Hall with knotted stomachs and high expectations.
Will our royal visitor be the prince of our dreams? Will Madame Ruby manage to contain herself in the presence of royalty? Will the prince be over the moon with year six's 'Clair de lune'? Will year four dance their way to a knighthood? Will year three drum up a royal storm? Will the year five sopranos reach such dizzying heights that only the royal corgis can hear them? Will the year one students rock L'Etoile to the rafters with their chart-worthy pop song? Which students will be awarded the special Founder's Day prizes and get to shake the Royal Hand? All will be revealed.
Good luck girls!
Yours, L'Etoilette

'Brilliant, Mimi,' Molly said, impressed. 'You're so good with words.'

'Right, I'm going on ahead,' Maria said, closing her laptop after uploading her article. 'I want to catch Mr Potts about a conductor's baton for you, Pippa, before he gets all flustered this morning.'

'Thanks so much!' Pippa said, now rushing about to get ready and go. 'I'd forgotten about that. Mind you, if I had my way, I'd stick with Faye's knitting needle. Call me superstitious, but it seems to have brought us luck so far!'

The dress rehearsal went as smoothly as could be expected considering it was being both run and attended by a bunch of headless chickens.

Fashion Faye had sensibly banned the girls from wearing their white stage outfits to the marquee lunch. And looking back, she had been wise. *Italian Tomato Soup*, followed by *Chicken Fajita Wraps* and *Chocolate Melting Middle Puddings* weren't the easiest foods to eat without leaving a trail of something down your front. But it did mean that they had to rush their food in order to nip back and change in time to be in their seats for 1:30 p.m. No student was willing to incur the wrath of Madame Ruby – or indeed any of the tetchy staff – for being late. It would mean immediate expulsion – or, in keeping with today's royal theme, 'Off with their heads'!

'Oh no!' Sally exclaimed, as the zip broke on her only pair of white jeans. It was at times like this when she wished she had a room-mate. Not Lucinda, of course, but just someone to share the jokes and the nightmares with. And this was definitely a nightmare! She grabbed her bag and bolted over to the girls' room to see if anyone could help.

'Molly!' Sally called, seeing Pippa and the twins in the corridor, looking angelic in their outfits.

'What's up, Sal?' Molly came running towards her. 'Oh no! What terrible timing – we've got about four minutes before we're thrown in the tower for being late. Let me think.'

'Think quickly!' Maria said. She had even bigger issues with being late than Madame Ruby did.

'I've got it!' Molly said and she dragged Sally back into the bedroom. 'We'll be one minute – don't you dare go without us!' she yelled through the door.

As Maria and Pippa shifted about nervously in the corridor, Sally re-emerged, looking like a Greek goddess.

'And you did all that in a minute?!' Pippa said, astounded.

'That had better not be my bed sheet you're wearing, Sally Sudbury!' Maria raised an eyebrow.

'No time for that,' Molly giggled. 'Anyway, she'll buy you a new one. That'll teach you for being so OCD and keeping an extra one, ready-ironed!'

But Maria was already halfway to the Kodak Hall, arriving with seconds to spare.

The Hall looked and smelled beautiful. There were garlands of flowers draped from the edges of the room up to a centre display, forming a kind of summer canopy. It felt magical. Suddenly, a fanfare sounded. Ripples of excitement spread around the room. It was the royal fanfare everyone had been dying to hear, marking the arrival of HRH.

As two big security guards opened the double doors at the back of the hall, Madame Ruby entered unaccompanied and made her way down the aisle – pausing slightly when she saw poor Sally dressed in what could only be described as an ancient Greek toga.

The fanfare sounded again. More footsteps were heard. Finally, the mystery royal made an entrance. As predicted and dreamed of by the vast majority in the room, it was indeed Prince Henry, second in line to the British throne.

The girls had been so determined not to react as if they were at a concert seeing one of their favourite boy bands for the first time, but alas, the sight of this young *Prince Charming* was too much for them to control their delight.

The room erupted into applause, with whoops and foot-stamping coming from all around, as Prince Henry made his way down the red-carpeted aisle to a velvet seat next to Madame Ruby, which she'd had ordered especially for his royal bottom alone.

Next to arrive was poor Mr Fuller and half a dozen more security guards. He wasn't the most extrovert of men at the best of times, so this pomp and ceremony made him want to die with embarrassment. Thankfully, Miss Hart was waiting on the stage to welcome him as guest speaker and had saved him a seat next to her.

The girls were in heaven. In those few moments, all their hopes and dreams had come true. They were not only in the presence of royalty, but a real live prince. It was truly going to be a day to remember.

'Your Royal Highness, L'Etoilettes, Ladies, Gentlemen,' Madame Ruby began, 'I am delighted to welcome you all to this very special Centenary Founder's Day service at L'Etoile, School for Stars. I think I speak for all of us, Your Royal Highness,' she turned and courtsied to Prince Henry, 'when I say how truly humbled and honoured we are, by your kindly agreeing to be with us today to share in the wonderful memories which will doubtless be with us for another one hundred years.' Everyone clapped and cheered again.

'And to you, Mr Fuller,' Madame Ruby turned to face him. 'We are entirely grateful to you too for the time you have taken out of your busy schedule to be with us today. I know the girls will each take away some precious advice about the industry from your speech and we are all very much looking forward to hearing your stories.' As she handed him the microphone and the rest of the school applauded, the Garland girls caught a look between Mr Fuller and Miss Hart, who was blushing with pride.

The next fifteen minutes while Emmett Fuller spoke were a blur to most of his audience. His tales, advice and anecdotes were both invaluable and entertaining, but he was well aware that he was far from the main attraction. But he didn't mind being the warm-up act. It was lovely for him to have been asked by Miss Hart, and for him to be part of something that was so important to her. He ended his speech by telling the girls to work hard and, most importantly, to believe in themselves and never to give up on their dreams. This struck a chord with everyone in the room – after all, the subject of most of their dreams was sitting before them on a velvet cushion – and they once again exploded with applause. Emmett Fuller took his seat, amused that he'd managed to connect with the girls in one way at least.

'Thank you for those wonderful words of wisdom, Mr Fuller,' Madame Ruby said. 'If any of our girls ever get the opportunity to work with you and your staff at Universal Music, they will indeed be in the best hands in the industry.'

Maria and Molly both nudged Pippa so hard at the same time, she nearly leapt out of her chair.

'And now to a part of the proceedings which is special to this particular Founder's Day Celebration. His Royal Highness, Prince Henry, has kindly agreed to present a select group of students with some awards, which my staff and I feel are most deserved.'

Another ripple of excitement travelled around the room. The atmosphere was electric with anticipation.

'Your Royal Highness, would you be so kind as to do the honours?'

14

A Royal Dream Comes True

As Prince Henry stood up to take the microphone, in his beautifully tailored navy-blue suit, crisp white shirt and tie, the girls gasped. He was even more wonderful in real life – and, standing there before them on that great stage, he looked more handsome and more regal than ever.

'Ladies,' he began.

'Ladies, he called us ladies . . .' Whispers echoed around the hall.

'It is my great pleasure to be with you on such a momentous day in the history of L'Etoile, School for Stars. And may I begin by saying how simply ravishing you all look?' More gasps.

'Ooooh, if he smiles in this direction one more time, I think I might faint,' squealed Molly as quietly as she could manage.

'And so to the business of the afternoon . . . the awards. I have here five awards for five very talented ladies. I believe Miss Hart is going to assist me and ensure I give the correct lady the correct award.' Miss Hart was blushing a shade of crimson now as she stood, ready and waiting to oblige.

'He said her name, the lucky thing!' Belle whispered. 'What I'd give to hear him say mine.'

'The first award is the *Most Inspiring All-Rounder Award* and goes, I believe, to a young lady in the fifth year who has continuously delivered the best performances in dance, singing and acting since joining L'Etoile.' Prince Henry looked up. 'Would Julia Knight please come and accept this award?'

The entire school turned to where the beautiful Julia was making her way to the stage.

'Ouch, that's like a knife in my beating heart,' exclaimed Molly again.

'Molly, will you pull yourself together,' said Maria. 'You're out of control. Of course all the prizes are going to go to the older girls. They've so much more experience than us first years. Now CO – or Mr Potts will throw you out. He's already looked over this way about four times for everyone to calm down.'

Molly did as she was told. Maria was pretty scary when she needed to be.

Julia courtsied, secretly thanking her lucky stars for all the ballet training that had made this moment so perfect. As she returned to her seat, amazingly unflustered and poised, the prince was already on to the next award.

Everyone held their breath again. It was like opening a chocolate wrapper to see if you had one of five golden tickets, knowing that there were now only four left to be claimed.

'Next to the *Critic's Choice Award*. This goes to a young lady who I'm told has received the most acclaim for her work and is already on the path to fame and fortune.'

'Oh, this has to go to Cissy Love!' Pippa whispered to Sally. 'She's just had her second play picked up by the Royal Theatre Company. Bet you any money it's her.'

'Would Cissy Love please come to the stage and accept her award?' Prince Henry announced.

'Told you!' Pippa cried, as the applause went up.

'Another fifth-year girl,' Molly groaned.

Cissy was slightly less poised than Julia had been, but who could blame her, as she bounded up to the stage and shook the Prince's hand. She blushed a shade of fuchsia pink as she made her way back to her seat, her face clashing with her red curly hair. Still, very well deserved, was the general consensus on her award.

The third award, the *Royal Philharmonic Award*, went to a third-year pianist called Jessica Ivory.

'Isn't Miss Ivory just the most wonderful name for a pianist?' Betsy cooed. 'And I have to say, she's absolutely mind-blowing to watch,' she continued, as Jessica thanked His Royal Highness and attempted a rather awkward courtsey.

Oh don't be too hard on her, Story-seeker. Courtseying doesn't come as naturally to pianists as it does to ballet dancers.

'The second to last award,' Prince Henry announced, 'is the *Composition Award*, and I'm told it goes to a student who has an extraordinary gift for songwriting.'

The room fell silent once again. There were a number of brilliant candidates for this award, most obviously, sixth-year student, Lucy Anthony, who had just had one of her compositions selected for the latest Walt Disney movie.

After a short pause, where he had deliberately allowed the room time to guess the winner, Prince Henry continued, 'And the award goes to a young lady who holds all the promise of being one of the greatest songwriters of our time. I believe we may even be hearing one of her compositions shortly.' The first years gasped in delight.

'Would Pippa Burrows please come and collect her award?'

Pippa was frozen to her seat. Molly threw her arms around her, genuinely over the moon for her friend. 'Pippa, it's you – he's talking about you!' And she shook her friend into consciousness. 'Up you get, Pips. Go and collect your award!'

Pippa started towards the stage, her face as white as her outfit. She couldn't believe it. First, her triumph at the Christmas gala, and now this. She must be dreaming. By the time she shook the Prince's hand and tried to courtsey, she was shaking like a leaf – all the time trying to make sure she didn't forget a single detail of what was happening. As she made her way back to her seat, she was grinning from ear to ear.

'Oh girls – she's so adorable,' Sally said to the twins.

'She has no idea how good she is, does she?'

'Such a lovely quality,' Maria agreed.

Pippa sat down to all of her friends patting her on the back and shoulders. She felt as though she'd truly won the lottery.

The prince waited for the happy reaction to die down a little before continuing.

'And so, ladies, to the final award of the day. This award is dedicated to the art of theatre, and its recipient, I'm told, is one of L'Etoile's most promising actresses. To make this award seem all the more deserved, it is accompanied by an invitation from Hollywood's top talent manager, Mr Calamity Mossback, for this young lady to attend an audition to star in the next Warner Brothers film.'

The whole school gasped again, knowing what an achievement it was to even be called up for that kind of casting.

'And the award goes to . . .' – the prince held his breath for what seemed like a lifetime – . '. . . Miss Molly Fitzfoster!' he announced.

Molly, who had been gossiping with Pippa and admiring her award, heard her name and gasped so loudly she nearly choked.

Maria jumped up, pulling her sister to her feet, and

gave her the biggest cuddle. 'Molly you've done it! Did you hear that?!'

'I . . . I . . .' Molly stammered in shock.

'Never mind that now – just get your little bottom up those steps and meet your prince!' Maria giggled, ecstatically happy for her sister.

Unlike Pippa, Molly didn't need to be told twice, and skipped over to the stage to claps and cheers. Older girls she didn't even know grabbed her arm as she went, congratulating her on the Warner Brothers audition. *What audition*? she thought, wishing she hadn't been so busy chatting. But she'd been so caught up in Pippa's happiness, she never dreamed she would be dealt the same wonderful luck.

As she climbed the stairs, to her utter horror, she caught her foot on the top step, but before she could tumble forward, a strong hand reached out and caught her arm, helping her up the rest of the way. Molly looked up and glowed with delight as she saw that it was the prince himself.

'Are you quite all right, Miss Fitzfoster?' he asked, gently. 'Congratulations on this wonderful achievement. And you must be so excited about your audition. I believe the appropriate term is *break a leg* – but not before you've even accepted the award, eh?'

The audience giggled and cooed. 'He just made a joke!' 'Did you hear that? Isn't he hilarious? Who'd have thought the prince would have such a sense of humour!'

'Oh thank you, Your Royal Highness,' Molly glowed, practically doing the splits as she performed the lowest courtsey she could. 'I am overwhelmed with pride and joy to have met you and to receive this award from you.'

As she walked back to her seat in a dreamlike trance, Molly Fitzfoster was sure she had just experienced the happiest moment of her life – past, present and future. How would she ever be able to top that?

♡

'Mollyyyyyy!' Maria shook her dumbstruck sister. 'You've got to snap out of this – or at least put this daydream on hold until after we've performed "Friends Forever". Have you forgotten you're leading the choir? The girls are relying on you!'

Something about the end of that speech jolted Molly back to reality. 'Oh, my goodness. I'd quite forgotten about our performance! I'm all of a dither!'

'You don't say,' Lydia laughed, as the first-year students stood huddled together backstage waiting for the fourth years' 'Royal Dance Medley' to finish.

'You can hardly blame her,' Belle whispered. 'I'm not sure I'd have made it to the stage if the prince had called my name out. In fact I'd probably be in the sick bay with Nurse Payne prodding me for signs of life!' The girls were relieved to laugh to release some of their nerves.

'Pippa are you all right – you look a bit traumatised too!' Sally asked.

'Don't say that. Do I? I'm fine – just feeling a bit of pressure having just won a songwriting award – and as soon as we sing "Friends Forever", everyone will be able to judge for themselves whether I deserve it or not!'

'You're a genius songwriter, Pippa! Would you do me a favour and start believing in yourself? We're going to smash it!' Maria winked.

And on that note, Madame Ruby announced the first years on stage.

'And finally, Your Royal Highness, a performance which encapsulates the very spirit of L'Etoile. The first years asked to appear as a single group choir and orchestra. They have chosen to perform a song written and composed by their own special *Composition Award* winner, Pippa Burrows. I give you "Friends Forever".'

The school fell silent as Pippa stepped on to the conductor's podium and raised her hand.

'Wait a minute . . . is that a knitting needle Pippa's conducting with, Helen?' Emmett Fuller whispered to Miss Hart.

Helen smiled and nodded. Funny, superstitious Pippa. She must have kept the knitting needle for luck, rather than exchange it for a proper baton.

The first years sang and played their hearts out for the prince, as though he was the only person in the room.

Ooooh . . . just little old me,
Ooooh . . . then we were three.

I can't explain the feeling,
The one that leaves me reeling.

I never thought that friends could be
A second kind of family,

Ooooh . . . this ain't no short-term endeavour
Ooooooh . . . you know we're friends forever . . .

As Lara brought down her drumstick with a

final crash of the cymbal, the whole school – staff, students, security and prince alike, were on their feet in rapturous applause.

The girls took their bows and hugged each other, each squealing with delight at the audience reaction. What a wonderful end to a wonderful ceremony!

They watched from the stage as the prince made his way out of the Kodak Hall to where his transport was waiting.

As soon as he was out of earshot, Miss Hart grabbed the microphone. 'Quickly everyone, would you please take up your positions along the driveway to wave His Royal Highness off. Safely though, please . . . try not to run each other down!'

But the girls were beyond listening and bolted out of the hall, desperate to catch one last glimpse of their Prince Charming before he disappeared from L'Etoile – and their lives – altogether.

'Have I missed him?' Betsy asked urgently, as she squirreled her way to the front for a better view.

'Not yet,' Molly answered, applying some smuggled blusher to her cheeks. 'But I think I can see the cars starting to move away now.'

The fanfares sounded for the last time as the first, second and third security cars drove past. It was easy to make out which car the prince was in, as his hand was waving from the window.

'He's coming, he's coming,' Sofia shouted.

The girls could no longer contain their emotion as the whole driveway exploded into a tunnel of whoops and cheers as they saluted the prince in their own way.

'Goodbye, Prince Henry. See you again in my dreams,' Molly said under her breath.

15

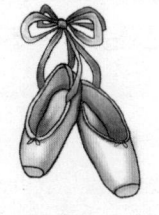

Calling Special Agents Fitzfoster and Burrows

Sadly, the Founder's Day fireworks were later cancelled, due to the fact that, after the prince's departure, the heavens had opened and it hadn't stopped raining for a second.

Frustratingly for the girls, this meant more time in class, writing up their memories from the day. Goodness only knows how the L'Etoile teaching staff managed to bring the girls back down to earth enough to get them to focus, but they did, and every classroom was buzzing with excited chatter.

Form 1 Alpha, with two recipients of the prince's special Founder's Day awards, was on an all-time high. The girls, including form tutor Mrs Spittleforth, crowded around Molly and Pippa, as they gave blow-by-blow accounts of their individual experiences with His Royal Highness.

While Maria outwardly appeared to be involved in the gossip of the day, her mind was a million miles away. As soon as the royal motorcade had disappeared from sight, Maria had bolted back to Garland to gather the Hart letter and photographs, neither of which she'd been able to hide under her white costume. She'd almost managed a full fifteen minutes thinking time to herself, before the rest of the house invaded to change back into their uniforms. The more she looked at Frank Hart's symbols alongside the photo of the L'Etoile main entrance hall, the more convinced she was that she knew exactly where to find the treasure. The only thing still a mystery to her was what the treasure would be. She decided in that moment that she couldn't possibly wait another day to find out the truth.

Maria Fitzfoster, and her team of investigators, would solve the mysterious *Legend of the Lost Rose* that very night.

'Molly . . . Molly . . . wake up,' Maria whispered, as she gently shook her sister at midnight.

Molly snuffled in her sleep and pulled the duvet over her head.

'Molly!' Maria repeated, poking her a little more forcefully this time.

'Wha . . . whatsssup?' Molly mumbled.

'It's time to solve a mystery!' Maria answered, excitedly. 'Pleeeease, Molly. Wake up!'

'Did someone call for a secret agent?' Pippa asked, giggling.

She leapt out of bed and stood posing like an assassin, dressed from head to toe in black lycra.

'Pippa, what are you wearing?!' Molly could hardly believe her eyes.

'And how did you know to be ready?' Maria said, aghast.

'I think I know you better than you know yourself, Agent Fitzfoster!' Pippa said, with a wink. 'I noticed you twitching all afternoon and sneaking looks at those old photos and knew it was only a matter of time before you'd have to investigate properly. So I went to bed prepared!'

'Didn't you just!' Maria said, laughing at Pippa. 'And you look like a proper spy, Agent Burrows.'

'And you will too by the time I've finished with us,'

said Molly, now wide awake with the excitement of getting to dress up. She flung a pair of black leggings and matching top over to Maria.

'You two are even crazier than I thought you were. Why has everything got to be such a drama?!' Maria said, exasperated. 'Oh all right then, but let's be quick about it.'

Four minutes later, the secret trio were creeping along the corridors of Garland, making their way to the entrance hall.

'What makes you so sure you've got this right?' Molly asked Maria after they successfully sneaked past Miss Coates' bedroom door without creaking a single floorboard.

'You'll see,' Maria answered. 'Now keep quiet until we get there, and follow my torch. I've deliberately put an almost dead battery in it so the glow isn't too bright. Thought it might show up under the bedroom doors as we go past. Last thing we need is for anyone to wake up. It's hard enough keeping three of us from being discovered, let alone if we have to take any of the others with us!'

Molly and Pippa obediently followed Maria. This was no time to get into a discussion.

As the girls approached the Garland door to the

quadrant which separated them from the main school, Pippa suddenly gasped.

'Oh girls, I've just thought . . . it's easy for us to get out of Garland, we can just wedge this door slightly so we can get back in later, but won't the back doors to L'Etoile be locked?'

'Oh no, she's right, Maria. Tell me you've already thought of that?' Molly asked, hopefully.

Maria shone the torch up under her chin so the girls could see her face. 'What do you take me for, an amateur?' she answered, insulted. 'Do you honestly think I haven't thought through every step of this route? Now chill out, the pair of you, or I'll go and solve this by myself. Just think of the glory headlines in the newspapers . . . *Maria Fitzfoster, Journalist and Super-Sleuth, Solves Legend of the Lost Rose – ALONE!'*

'I was only saying!' Pippa said, a little hurt. 'Maybe you need to CO!'

Molly giggled.

Maria realised she'd got a bit carried away with herself. 'OK, I hear you. I'm sorry. I think the adrenalin is starting to flow now. You know I can't do this without you . . . either of you. I'm blinking terrified of the dark if the truth be known, but please, would you just trust me? And no more questions; we're wasting valuable mystery-solving time.'

'Agreed,' Pippa nodded. 'Lead the way, Agent F1.'

'F1?' Molly asked, confused.

'Yes – there's two of you aren't there? Maria's Agent Fitzfoster 1 and you're . . .'

'Will you come on!' said Maria, agitated, from halfway across the quad.

'Is that doorstop firmly fixed, Pips?' Molly said before they left the safety of Garland. 'I'd die if we couldn't get back in.'

Pippa gave it a good wiggle. 'Yep!' she whispered back. 'Come on, before your sister bursts a blood vessel.'

♡

As Agent B and Agent F2 approached L'Etoile, they made out the dimly-lit silhouette of Agent F1 scrabbling around in the bushes by the doors.

'Mimi, what are you doing?' Molly asked and then shivered. 'Oh my goodness, it's absolutely freeeeezing out here!'

'It should be just over . . . ah, here we are.' Maria produced a plastic box from behind one of the tall holly bushes. Pulling a hairpin from her bun, as she'd seen in so many movies, she wiggled it in the lock and, to her relief, the lid popped open and a silver key dropped out onto the earth below.

'One back-door key!' Maria announced.

'But how did you know . . .' Pippa said, her teeth chattering as she spoke.

'Probably best not to ask, Pips. What you don't know can't hurt you! I'm not sure breaking and entering is something you want to add to your list of achievements,' Maria answered.

The truth, in fact, wasn't as exciting as the mystery . . . more a stroke of luck, Story-seeker. Back in the days of TTD, Maria had seen Mr Hart lock the back door and hide the emergency key. She just knew that little discovery would come in useful one day! The only risky bit was whether the hairpin trick would actually work in real life. She didn't mention she'd been practising on the lock on Molly's diary!

♡

By the time the trio entered the main L'Etoile building, their hearts were beating out of their chests. Fear and excitement now consumed them as they suddenly realised the seriousness of what they were up to.

'Come on, girls,' Maria said, seeing how pale Molly and Pippa looked. 'We're so nearly there. Just one more hurdle to get past before we reach the entrance hall.'

Pippa looked alarmed.

'Oh no, I forgot about Madame Ruby!' Molly groaned.

As bad luck would have it, Madame Ruby's living quarters were located directly above the main entrance hall, in a corridor off the staircase.

'We'll just have to be quiet as mice and only talk if it's absolutely necessary,' Maria said. Molly and Pippa nodded in silence.

The girls made their way along the main corridor, passing all the empty classrooms as they went. Molly wondered how somewhere so wonderful could be so unbelievably creepy in the dark.

'As we're getting near the hall, try to follow in my footsteps,' Maria said. 'I've planned this route carefully, I know where all the creaky floorboards are. The slightest sound will echo like mad and we don't want to wake you-know-who!'

At that moment, the faint sound of music drifted down the corridor.

'I think you-know-who might still be awake!' Pippa whispered in alarm.

Maria hadn't seen that one coming! It was nearly one o'clock in the morning, for goodness' sake. What was Madame Ruby still doing up?

'Right, the way I see it, we have two choices. Either we turn back now and try again tomorrow. Or we carry on as planned, and I for one say we go for it. We've come too far to waste this chance. Come on, you two, what do you say?'

Pippa couldn't remember ever having felt so terrified. But as she looked at Molly for support, she saw she was on her own.

'Nothing ventured, nothing gained and all that,' she said as cheerfully as she could. 'I just hope Madame Ruby's not in the habit of walking the corridors at night!'

'Don't, Pippa! Oh, Mimi, she wouldn't . . . I mean, why would she?' Molly stammered, but Maria was already making her way by torchlight along the corridor towards the entrance hall.

As the girls reached the little door under the staircase, they could hear Madame Ruby's music system, clear as a bell, belting out Michael Bublé.

'You two stay here for a sec while I check the coast

is clear,' Maria ordered. She switched off her torch, as there was plenty of light flooding the hall from the corridor above.

'Is she crazy?' Pippa said, watching Maria make her way up the staircase above them. 'I thought we were avoiding that area like the plague!'

'She's got to make sure Madame Ruby's actually in her apartment, before we start creeping about. That's our only hope of making sure we don't get caught,' Molly said.

'That sister of yours must have nerves of steel!' Pippa whispered. 'My heart can beat louder than Michael Bublé can sing, that's for sure.'

'Me too, Pips! But you have to admit . . . it's exciting too. Just think what a story we'll have to tell our grandchildren. We're about to make the history books if we solve this mystery, like Maria says we're going to.'

Pippa managed a smile but, really and truthfully, she wished Agent Burrows was still safely tucked up in bed!

16

A Night to Remember

$\mathcal{M}$aria had never felt so alive. As she mounted the staircase, careful to avoid every creaky patch on the way, she felt the adrenalin rush through her body. Tiptoeing down the corridor, she could see clearly that one of the apartment doors was ajar, which was why they could hear the music. Maria wondered if she dare pop her head inside to check whether Madame Ruby was there.

She took a deep breath and gently eased the door open enough to see through it. What a beautiful room, decorated wall to wall with mirrors. Suddenly, she saw the reflection of Madame Ruby, in a long cream silk dressing-gown, dancing around, with a champagne glass in one hand and a fan in the other. Maria had to smile, but didn't hang around. She'd checked what she needed to check. Now just one query remained: should she silently close the door on the way out? At least, that way, the girls might hear or see a glow if Madame Ruby re-opened it. Yes, she'd close it. And with the utmost care, Maria scurried back to the entrance hall to rejoin Molly and Pippa.

'Oh, thank goodness!' Molly squeezed Maria. 'We were starting to get a bit worried.'

'What happened? Was she up there?' Pippa asked.

'Yes, dancing around without a care in the world. I think she may have had one too many glasses of champagne! One of the doors to the corridor was open, which is where the music and light were coming from – but I've closed it now. At least we'll know if she opens the door again if we suddenly hear the music and see the lights.'

'Well done, Mimi! Now let's find this blinkin' treasure!'

Maria turned the torch back on, as they'd lost the light from upstairs when she'd closed the door.

'Let's start with our backs to the front door as if we'd just come in under the star in the porch, seeing as that's where the clues begin.'

Maria shone a light on Frank's symbols.

⇧ ⬇ ■ 7 ⇨ ☐ 4 ⇧ ■ 9 ⇦ ■ 5 ⇧ ■ 2 ⇨ ☐ ⇧ 🔥 ☉

'Right, so the first two we've done – the look up at the star part. Then I reckon the arrow down is telling us to look down.'

The girls looked down at the floor. It was just like the photo, a huge chessboard of black and white tiles.

'Are you thinking what I'm thinking?' Molly asked. 'The next symbol, the black square, is this centre black tile as you come in the L'Etoile doors under the star knocker.'

'Exactly,' Maria grinned with glee.

'So what you're saying is, using this black tile as number one, we need to count seven tiles to our right and we should reach a white tile like the next three symbols show,' Pippa said, starting to enjoy herself a little.

'Exactly,' Maria said again, loving every minute of sharing her discovery.

The girls counted seven tiles to the right and came to a white tile. Looking at the symbols again, they counted four tiles forward and stopped on a black tile.

'I can't believe this is happening!' Molly whispered.

'Don't stop now, Moll,' Maria said.

They followed the next couple of symbol instructions . . . nine tiles to the left to black. Stop. Five tiles forward to black. Stop. Two tiles to the right to white. Stop.

'Now what?' Molly asked.

'There's a forward arrow but no number to say how many – just a flame symbol – it must be the fire!' Pippa whispered back, confused.

Even Maria was quiet. She'd expected the answer to be so obvious once they'd got this far. The three girls looked at the enormous fireplace in front of them, following the beam of Maria's torch as it hovered over every inch, desperately searching for treasure. She came to rest upon Lola Rose's lovely face in the oil painting, which hung above it.

'We must be so close!' Maria whispered, puzzled. 'What is it that we're not seeing?'

Pippa and Molly had nothing to offer. They were all stumped.

'Let's go back to the symbols. We must have missed something vital and made a wrong move somewhere.'

Molly was looking back to the front entrance, counting the tiles again to check they'd counted correctly.

'One thing's for certain, we're in the right place. It's just when we got to the next forward arrow and the flame symbol that it seems to have gone wrong.'

Pippa was looking around and suddenly grabbed Frank's letter to check something. 'What if it's not a forward arrow at all . . . and what if the flame isn't the fireplace?'

'I don't follow you, Pips,' Molly said, even more confused.

'She's right!' Maria struggled to keep her delight to a whisper. 'Go on, Pippa . . . go on!'

'What if it's an arrow *up*, not *forward* – like the first arrow was to look up at the star. And the flame is for *candlelight*, not *firelight*!'

The trio stared up to the ceiling from where they were standing and there, hanging in all its glory, was the enormous crystal chandelier.

'No way. Of course . . . the chandelier! That would have been lit by candlelight at the turn of the century,' Molly answered, scanning the huge crystal light fitting above. 'What's it made of – diamonds or something?'

'Not quite, Moll,' Maria answered. 'But you're not far off. Look again.' And this time, Maria shone her torch up at the central ball, which hung slightly lower than the rest of the chandelier.

Pippa and Molly gasped.

There, twinkling inside the crystal ball, as the symbol of the dot within a circle showed, was the biggest, reddest ruby you have ever seen or imagined.

'The lost rose!' Molly whispered. 'Of course, it had to be a ruby! It's the most precious interpretation of a rose you could possibly find.'

'How romantic!' Pippa added.

'And how clever. Until now, it's been for Lola Rose's eyes only, under the gaze of her portrait,' said Maria as she held up her camera phone to take a photo of it.

CREEEAAAAK!

The girls jumped out of their skin. They hadn't realised how silent it had been until there was a sudden noise.

Without uttering a word, Maria took charge and whisked them all through the door under the staircase, along the classroom corridor, still being careful to avoid any creaky boards, and out of the back door into the courtyard. Their silence continued as Maria locked up and replaced the key. They sneaked back into the safety of their room at Garland, as quietly as they'd left it all those hours ago, still not knowing whether it was safe to speak.

'Can I breathe yet?' Molly said, breaking the silence.

'What was that noise?!' Pippa puffed. 'Do you think someone was watching us? Oh my gosh, I so hope not. That just would be the worst ending to the best day of my life.'

'I've been thinking about that all the way back and I really don't think there can have been. I think it might have been one of the floorboards re-releasing from where I trod it down earlier,' Maria answered. 'If there was someone there, I'm sure we'd have heard more than just that one little creak. There can't possibly be anyone else at L'Etoile who knows more about the location of those creaky boards than me!'

'Are you absolutely sure, Mimi?'

'What else can I say, Moll?' Maria answered. 'I can't be a hundred per cent sure, but I'm ninety-nine per cent convinced there's nothing to worry about. Anyway, never mind things that go bump in the night. Can we talk about what just happened?'

'It's like a dream,' Pippa answered.

'Are you kidding, Pips? The size of that ruby was no dream, let me tell you. It was blinding, even in the nearly-dead light of my little torch.'

'I just can't believe no one's spotted it before now,' said Molly. 'It's extraordinary. I mean, does no one ever clean that chandelier, for goodness' sake? They couldn't miss it!'

'Probably, but without Frank's letter and clues, you'd never in a million years believe that was a real ruby suspended in that crystal ball. You'd just think it was a beautiful piece of glass.'

'Well, I think it's the most beautiful thing I've ever seen. A heart at the heart of L'Etoile; joining her mistress in watching over all who pass under her.'

Maria giggled softly. 'You are sweet, Molly. But when you've finished being soppy, have a think about what we should do with this discovery. Don't forget the last part of Frank Hart's letter about returning the lost rose to its rightful owner. That's something we really need to think about.'

'OK, Mimi, but not tonight, eh? I'm practically sleep-talking right now. Let's get some kip and look at it with fresh eyes in the morning. Night, Agent Fitzfoster 1. Night, Agent Burrows,' Molly said yawning.

The trio didn't even make it out of their secret agent outfits before passing out under their duvets.

What a night of adventure, Story-seeker!

17

Making the Right Decision

The excitement of Founder's Day itself and
the sleepless night of anticipation which had
preceded it had left the entire school badly in need of
a lie-in the following morning – and there wasn't a
student at L'Etoile who needed an extra few hours in
bed that morning more than our midnight-mystery-
solving trio.

As the morning bell sounded at 9 a.m., Maria sat
bolt upright.

'We have to tell Miss Hart!' she announced.

'Eh? What time is it?' Pippa said, scrabbling around
for her watch.

'Nine o'clock. We've got an hour before classes start

this morning. I say we go via Miss Hart's office. I've been dreaming about what to do and we simply have to tell her that we've found her inheritance.'

'Oh, Mimi, are you absolutely sure that's the right way to play this? I mean, there will be a media storm around L'Etoile *and* poor Miss Hart, once this gets out,' Molly said.

'I'm with Maria on this, Moll,' said Pippa, reaching for her toothbrush. 'Besides, what if we are already not the only people who know about the existence and the location of the *Lost Rose*? I still can't shake the terrible feeling that we weren't alone last night. It would be a total nightmare for someone else to let the cat out of the bag before we've had the chance to . . . or worse, steal the jewel for themselves.'

'Maybe you're right. What have we got first this morning?' Molly asked.

'We're back in our form classes until lunchtime to finish writing up our Founder's Day memory reports,' answered Maria.

'I tell you what then, why don't I go straight to class and explain to Miss Spittleforth that you two have a meeting with Miss Hart this morning. Don't want to raise any suspicions by all three of us not turning up without any explanation,' Pippa offered.

'I think that's a very sensible and unselfish idea, Pips – if you don't mind not being there at the meeting.'

'Not at all. This is your mystery and your big moment anyway, Maria. You've done all the legwork on this one. Go for it, Fitzfosters!'

♡

'Come in!' Miss Hart called, as the twins knocked on her office door shortly before 10 o'clock.

'Good morning, ladies,' she said as Molly and Maria trotted in. 'And many congratulations, Molly, on your wonderful award yesterday. You must be simply beside yourself with excitement for your film audition.'

Molly had to think back for a second. With everything that had gone on since Prince Henry had left L'Etoile, she'd quite forgotten about her forthcoming audition for Warner Brothers.

'Thank you so much, Miss. Yes, I'm absolutely over the moon, as you say.' Miss Hart motioned to the girls to take a seat. 'But actually, Maria and I have come to see you for an entirely different reason this morning.'

'Oh yes?' Miss Hart looked suspiciously at the girls. *What could they possibly be up to now? There simply hadn't been time for mischief around the royal visit. Or had there?*

'Mimi, you start and I'll fill in anything you miss out. You're so much better with the facts than I am. I'll just turn the whole story into a melodrama.'

Sensing that the girls had something serious to tell her, Miss Hart came round from her side of the desk and sat down on the sofa opposite them to relax the atmosphere.

No sooner had Maria taken a breath, than the whole story came tumbling out. She left nothing out, starting from her hacking into Luscious Tangerella's online article for the *London Gazette* about Frank and Lola's relationship and *The Legend of the Lost Rose*; to Twinkle's arrival at L'Etoile as Garland's secret housemate; to getting caught by Miss Hart's father and him agreeing to look after Twinkle; to their discovery of Frank Hart's letter concealed within the pages of her father's book; to their decoding of the clues; to their ultimate discovery of the location of Frank's hidden treasure.

By the end, Miss Hart was completely speechless. What alarmed her most about the whole story was that she clearly had no idea what these girls were capable of. There was a part of her that was secretly very impressed, but she remained in turmoil about how to handle the situation, given that some fairly fundamental L'Etoile rules had been broken. She was the deputy head after all, and had a duty to maintain some sort of discipline at the school. But then, how could she scold them when they'd been so unbelievably clever? Particularly, as the whole adventure was so personal to her and the Hart family. This was going to be a tough one.

As Miss Hart went to speak, Maria jumped in quickly. 'And the last thing we need to tell you – sorry for interrupting, Miss – which is in fact our whole reason for coming to you this morning, is that it's all yours, Miss Hart,' Maria said, a look of relief spreading across her face.

This stopped Miss Hart in her tracks, and whatever she had apparently been about to say went quite out of her mind. 'I'm sorry,' she said, confused. 'I don't follow you. What could this all possibly have to do with me?' she asked, innocently as a child.

'Mimi, why don't you show her Frank's letter so Miss Hart can see for herself?' Molly suggested.

Maria pulled the letter out from her sleeve for the last time, and held it out for Miss Hart. As she read, everything became clear.

To Whom It May Concern,

If you are reading this, I accept that the time has come for the beauty of my rose to share itself with you and perhaps with the rest of the world. In return, I ask that you make one vow: that, upon discovery of my rose, you do not keep it for yourself, but you ensure that it is returned to the last lady of my line. If you choose to ignore my wishes, you will be cursed to lead a life without love and, believe me, there is no worse punishment.

Yours,

Frank Hart

'Well, my goodness me,' Miss Hart muttered, turning the single page over in her hands. 'I see now what you mean.'

Then her attention was drawn to the symbols the girls had spoken of:-

⇧ ⬇ ■ 7 ⇨ ▢ 4 ⇧ ■ 9 ⇦ ■ 5 ⇧ ■ 2 ⇨ ▢ ⇧ 🔥 ☉

'However did you know where to begin with solving these clues?' she asked, more dumbfounded than ever.

Molly and Maria grinned at each other.

'Let's just say that without Molly's natural talent for

tripping up wherever she goes, we wouldn't have had the foggiest idea where to start,' Maria said, as Molly first looked horrified and then saw the funny side of that comment, picturing herself lying spread-eagled across the threshold to L'Etoile.

'It all starts below the L'Etoile star knocker on the main entrance doors,' said Maria. 'Actually, Miss Hart,' she continued in earnest. 'If you have time now, it really would be better to show you, clue by clue. It's so exciting. May we?'

♡

Moments later, the twins were walking Miss Hart through each symbol in the main entrance hall. While Maria had spilled the beans on just about everything that had led the girls to solving the *Legend of the Lost Rose*, she'd not actually given the exact location of the stone away – nor had she said it was a ruby. They'd just said they'd found Frank Hart's precious hidden treasure for Lola Rose and that it now rightfully belonged to Miss Hart. She was in for the surprise of her life!

'And this is the only point we got wrong to begin with,' Maria explained as they came to a halt beneath the chandelier.

'Yes,' Molly jumped in. 'We presumed that this

arrow, followed by a flame, ⇑ 🔥 ☉ meant move or look *forwards* like the previous arrows did – the flame symbol representing the fireplace . . .'

'. . . but what it actually meant,' Maria jumped back in, determined to finish the story, '. . . was to look *upwards*, not *forwards* . . . at the chandelier. Luckily we realised there would have been real candles providing the lighting when Frank wrote these clues, not electric bulbs as there are now.'

'Yes, I see. How very clever of you,' said Miss Hart in admiration.

'Now, are you ready?' Maria asked Miss Hart and Molly. They both nodded.

'3-2-1 – look up!' she commanded, triumphantly. At which point both she and Molly gasped in horror.

'I-i-i-i-it's gone, Mimi!' Molly stammered.

Maria was stunned into silence.

'Oh, Miss Hart, it was there, we absolutely promise. We haven't led you on a wild-goose chase, honest!' Molly cried in desperation.

'There must have been someone here watching last night, just as we feared,' Maria said. 'But how could they have stolen it?'

'Now slow down, girls. What exactly is it that's missing?' Miss Hart asked.

But Molly was beside herself. 'Oh, Mimi, I feel awful. Lola Rose's treasure has been there for over a century, keeping watch over L'Etoile, and now it's been taken, all because of our stupid curiosity!'

'Maria, are you absolutely sure about all this?' Miss Hart asked. 'I mean, you say you only discovered all of this by torchlight last night. You said yourself the battery was nearly dead. The mind can play tricks as you well know – and never more so than in the dark.'

Maria was mortified that Miss Hart might doubt their story. How could this have happened – and so quickly too? It was only a few hours ago that they had stood there in very different circumstances, basking in the light of the glittering red stone.

'But we all saw it!' she cried. 'All three of our minds couldn't have played the same trick. It's just impossible.'

Molly suddenly came back to life. 'Mimi, your phone! You took a picture on your phone . . . just before we were scared away by that noise on the stairs . . . remember?!'

Maria grinned. She'd totally forgotten she'd done that. Quickly, she pulled out her mobile – ignoring a faint frown from Miss Hart for having a phone in her possession during school hours.

'Thank goodness! Here!' she announced and thrust the phone into Miss Hart's hand.

And sure enough, Miss Hart saw a red glow coming from the central crystal ball, a central ball that was no longer hanging from the chandelier.

'A ruby?' she gasped, looking at the twins in astonishment.

'The biggest ruby you've ever seen Miss Hart. Red as the reddest rose, from Frank to his Lola Rose,' Molly confirmed, dreamily.

'How unbelievably beautiful,' Miss Hart muttered, her eyes darting between the photograph and then the empty space directly above.

♡

'UNDENIABLY BEAUTIFUL INDEED,' came a voice from the shadows. Miss Hart and the girls swung round so fast that the phone clattered to the floor.

'Madame Ruby . . .' Miss Hart began, feeling like a naughty student herself. 'Maria and Molly Fitzfoster have just been telling me the most unbelievable . . .'

'Silence!' Madame Ruby snapped. And the trio shuddered.

'I am well aware what these thieving little monsters

have been up to – creeping around in the dead of night, attempting to steal my property. I just didn't expect the third criminal to be you, Helen, dear.'

'But—' Maria tried to explain.

'I said, silence!' Madame Ruby snapped again.

'Now that's quite enough!' Helen Hart exploded, much to the twins' surprise. She had always been so timid around the dominant headmistress. Even Madame Ruby looked as if she had been physically punched by Miss Hart's unexpected response.

'I beg your pardon, Miss Hart?' the headmistress said, in a controlled voice.

'I . . . I said that's enough,' Miss Hart continued slightly less confidently. 'That is, it would be far preferable to continue this discussion in your office, without the girls being present, if you don't mind, Madame Ruby. I'm not sure what you are suggesting with regard to my being here with these ladies but, I can assure you, I heard this incredible tale for the first time this morning.'

'It's true . . .' Molly said, plucking up the courage to defend Miss Hart, but she was shot down with a glare.

'Miss Hart had nothing to do with us being here last night,' Maria said suddenly. Nothing made her angrier than seeing Molly upset.

'I'm not going to say who the third person with us last night was, but I can assure you it wasn't Miss Hart. It's all happened exactly as she said. We had no intention of stealing anything . . . and the proof of that is our reporting our findings to Miss Hart as soon as we were able to this morning.'

Helen Hart was shocked and touched by the courage of the girls.

'I can see that perhaps I have been hasty,' Madame Ruby answered, a little more softly. 'But please do not underestimate the stress I have been subjected to, being disturbed in the dead of night and discovering my school being burgled by torchlight. I would have confronted you on the spot if I had realised you were students, but I couldn't be sure of my own safety. You could have been armed gunmen for all I knew.'

Molly and Maria felt awful. As much as Madame Ruby wasn't in their list of top ten favourite people, they did feel bad at the thought of having frightened her silly. They hadn't considered how their actions might affect someone discovering them in the middle of the night.

'We are sorry, Madame Ruby. We never meant to cause you any distress. I guess we were so focused on solving the mystery of the *Lost Rose*, that we didn't really consider anything else,' Maria said.

'None of it matters anyway,' Molly said, glumly. 'The rose really has been stolen now – and goodness knows by who. We'll never get it back.'

'I presume that this is what you are referring to?' Madame Ruby said as she pulled out a glistening crystal ball from her pocket.

Miss Hart and the twins gasped as the ball flashed ruby red as the light caught the stone within.

'Of course!' Maria explained, kicking herself for not realising there wasn't some mysterious third-party burglar, just the Grand Madame herself.

'Oh my!' gasped Miss Hart, as she caught her first glimpse of the lost treasure.

Madame Ruby continued to explain.

'My curiosity was drawn when I noticed that the door to my apartment had been closed at some point during the evening. I'd left it open deliberately, you see, to air some paint fumes which were lingering following Mr Hart's repair work to the hall stand. As soon as I spotted torchlight darting around the L'Etoile entrance hall and heard muffled whispers, I immediately sought a hiding place from where I could observe what I thought was my school being burgled. I'd be lying if I didn't say I was completely petrified of being discovered. Unfortunately for me, I hit a creaky floorboard, which was thankfully enough to frighten the intruders off, but before I'd got a good look at them.

'Finally, I plucked up the courage to go downstairs and see what had been taken. I knew the focal point had been around the chandelier so stood below it trying to work out what had been taken. Then suddenly I spotted the red stone, glittering inside the central ball of the chandelier and put two and two together about the legend surrounding my great-grandmother. I couldn't believe I hadn't spotted it before now, having spent my whole life in these corridors.'

Molly and Maria and Miss Hart were enthralled by Madame Ruby's version of events as she continued her story.

'I wasn't even sure if the jewel was real but thought I should fetch Mr Hart's ladder and unhook the central ball for safekeeping. After all, the school had already been broken into once. Who was to say there wouldn't be another attempt before the morning? But tell me, L'Etoilettes, I am very interested to know how you came to be so very well informed about the *Legend of the Lost Rose* and its location.'

Maria grinned with pride, while Molly looked terrified.

'Madame Ruby,' Miss Hart interrupted, her turn to defend her girls. 'I think that perhaps we ought to retire to your office and I will explain the whole story, while the girls go back to class. It's been quite a morning, and Miss Spittleforth will think they've been abducted!'

'Heaven forbid,' Madame Ruby said. 'Off you go, girls. And thank you . . . I think.'

As Molly and Maria ran off to class, they didn't know how to feel. None of this had played out quite like they'd thought it would.

'I just can't wait to see the look on old Ruby's face when Miss Hart shows her the letter where Frank writes that the treasure is hers. Can you imagine?'

Molly's eyes widened with excitement. Oh, to be a fly on that office wall.

18

A Heart to Hart

Upstairs in the headmistress's office, Miss Hart retold the girls' story, just as they'd told it to her earlier that morning. She, loyally, left out a couple of details which might get both the girls and her father into trouble, mainly the story of how Twinkle came to be at L'Etoile!

'My sincere apologies, Helen, for jumping to inappropriate conclusions in front of the girls,' Madame Ruby said, as she poured Miss Hart a fresh coffee.

'I just don't know what came over me. I can only claim that the lack of sleep, shock and adrenalin at what happened overnight has left me quite out of sorts this morning.'

Helen Hart couldn't believe her ears. Never mind the fact that she had actually apologised for something, Madame Ruby had never been this civil and honest with her in her life. All those years she had spent growing up at L'Etoile, under the care of her father and Madame Ruby's mother, Amber Rose, she'd been like the annoying younger sister Madame Ruby had never asked for, and that resentment had continued well into adulthood.

'It's forgotten, Ruby,' Miss Hart said, warmed by this new level of communication they were sharing. 'What is important now, is to discuss what we should do with the *Lost Rose*.'

'Of course it is,' Madame Ruby snapped, sounding more like her usual self. Her face had been a picture when Miss Hart showed her the letter that said that she was the rightful owner of the jewel.

'I'm presuming you'll want to sell the ruby and disappear off round the world with Emmett,' she continued, grumpily. 'And I can't say I would blame you. A jewel of that size with such a history attached to it would most certainly be priceless at auction. You'd be wealthy beyond your wildest dreams.'

'Yes, that option has crossed my mind,' Miss Hart answered. 'But . . .'

'Yes?' Madame Ruby said quickly, looking desperately hopeful.

'But . . .' Miss Hart continued, 'as much as the ruby appears to be mine on paper, I can't help but believe it truly belongs where it was so lovingly laid to rest all those years ago . . . at the heart of L'Etoile.'

'Oh yes, Helen, yes,' Madame Ruby was uncharacteristically animated. 'I quite agree with you.'

Helen Hart was stunned to experience this side to Ruby after years of getting the cold shoulder. But she had a plan to share.

'I don't know what you would feel about this, but I think that the wonderful story of my great-grandfather Frank Hart and your great-grandmother, Lola Rose D'Arcy, and the *Legend of the Lost Rose* should be shared with the whole world.' She took a breath.

'I was thinking that perhaps we could allow Molly and Maria to grant Luscious Tangerella, the *London Gazette* journalist, an interview, which we would closely control, of course. We could use that interview as a fantastic advertisement for the school, where we also announce that starting this summer holidays, the school's doors would be opened for six weeks for visitors – paying ones, of course – to come and learn about our history. As part of their experience they would all be given the clues from Frank's letter and be guided to making their own discovery of the *Lost Rose*, which will be put back in its usual place for all to see. What do you think?'

'I think that's a marvellous idea, Helen. A most unselfish approach and very generous of you. I would like to think I would have done the same thing in your situation. The revenue from these summer tours will help us to make L'Etoile even bigger and better than it already is.'

'To L'Etoile, then.' Miss Hart held out her coffee cup to toast the school.

'To L'Etoile,' Madame Ruby repeated softly.

'And don't worry about security for the stone. I've just the thing!' Miss Hart smiled, picturing Twinkle as the new protector of the *Lost Rose*, keeping watch from a throne-shaped dog bed placed directly below the chandelier.

19

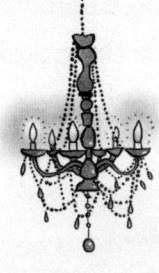

Another Adventure Comes to an End

'What a term!' Pippa exclaimed after the twins had finished updating her on what had happened with Miss Hart that morning. 'I just can't believe it! You couldn't make it up if you tried.'

'Tell me about it!' cried Molly. 'I nearly died when Madame Ruby suddenly appeared behind us. Never mind the Warner Brothers audition! I felt as though I was in a film this morning. I wonder what's going on in that meeting and what, if anything, has been decided.'

'Hopefully we'll find out soon. I reckon we should still keep this whole thing to ourselves for the time being though. It's not really our secret to share any more, is it?' said Maria, secretly desperate to let *Yours, L'Etoilette* blow the whole thing wide open in her blog.

'I reckon you're right. It'll all depend on what Miss Hart wants to do with the *Lost Rose*. She might just want to sell it – maybe Dad would buy it!' Molly wondered. 'Although I don't think that's very Miss Hart, to be honest. I just can't imagine her wanting to part with it – not for any sum of money.'

'You're absolutely right. She's far more likely to recommend loaning it to a museum or something so the world can see it. It does deserve to be seen by as many people as possible. It's so beautiful. I can't wait to see it again properly in daylight,' Pippa answered.

'It would be such a shame for it to leave L'Etoile. I almost wish we hadn't discovered it. If it did get taken away, I'd feel as though we'd let Frank and Lola down somehow. It belongs here,' Molly sighed.

'What will be, will be, girls. We just have to hope the Grand Madame and Miss Hart make the right decision . . . if they can agree!' she giggled. 'They might have killed each other by now over this! Come on, let's go down to supper. Having missed breakfast and lunch, I can't remember the last time I had more than a handful of cola bottles as opposed to a proper hot meal . . . even if it is a Mackle the Jackal special!'

'I wonder when this arrived?' Molly asked, spotting an envelope on the floor by the door to their room.

Molly turned it over and read 'Strictly Private: Maria & Molly Fitzfoster'. Then she noticed the small D'Arcy family crest in the top right-hand corner, with the words 'From the Headmistress's Office' in a neat font below.

'This could go one of two ways, girls,' Maria gulped, fearing the worst.

'If I'm really honest, I'm feeling pretty pleased my name isn't on that envelope,' Pippa said, a relieved look on her face. 'I ended the first term in a bit of hot water – just imagine how much trouble I'd be in two terms in a row.'

'Oh girls, have a little faith. How bad can it be?' the ever-optimistic Molly answered, tearing open the envelope.

'You just had to ask and tempt fate, didn't you!' Maria cried in alarm. 'I can't bear it. Go on, Moll. What does it say?'

Dear Maria & Molly,

Firstly I would like to start by thanking you both for your honesty earlier today.

HOWEVER, as you are only too aware, the events of last night were highly irregular and rules were broken which cannot go unpunished.

'Oh here we go,' Maria groaned, but Molly continued, unfazed.

HOWEVER ... given the wonderful nature of your discovery, I have decided to overlook the bad behaviour on this occasion in favour of channelling both my, and your, energies into a far more worthwhile activity.

Miss Hart, as the undeniable heir to the Lost Rose, has kindly insisted that the stone should remain at L'Etoile in its rightful resting place, and that visitors should be able to come during the summer holidays and partake in their own historical treasure-hunt of sorts. As both punishment and thanks, we would very much like for you both – and for the third party who was present on the evening in question – Miss Burrows, I suspect – to join us in making plans for this suggested summer 'Lost Rose of L'Etoile Mystery Tour', which we hope will become a legendary experience in itself. We would like to start the ball rolling by granting an interview to Luscious Tangerella from the London Gazette, who, I am told, was instrumental in your journey to discover the truth. Miss Tangerella will be in my office at 10 a.m. tomorrow morning and we would like the three of you to be there.

I trust you have no objections and will see you in the morning.

Madame Ruby Rose D'Arcy

Ps. Please do keep this whole affair to yourselves until I make an official announcement.

'Errrr . . . did she really just say all that?' Molly cried.

'Errrr . . . did I really just get busted again?' Pippa asked in disbelief.

'Errrr . . . would you two get a grip. This is brilliant!' Maria squealed, throwing a pillow in each direction. 'I can't believe I'm actually going to meet Luscious Tangerella. Moll, can you believe it?'

'I'm just so pleased for you, Mimi,' Molly answered. 'You sooo deserve it too. Finally, something has come along that's right up your street, rather than you always taking the path that's best for me, so we can be together.'

Maria looked amazed at her sister and then hugged her hard. Sometimes she really did misjudge her. Not in a bad way, but times like this reminded her not to underestimate how clever Molly was, underneath all the curlers and lipgloss.

'I just can't believe we're not in a world of trouble! What a result – and what a great idea about getting visitors in over the summer. I'd so pay to come and relive our adventure, wouldn't you?'

'Absolutely,' said Maria. 'I might write up some notes about the order in which everything happened – so we get our story straight tomorrow. I'll die if we mess up in front of Miss Tangerella. I would love this little introduction to actually lead to something concrete for me when I leave school. Wouldn't it just be amazing if she gave me a job eventually?'

'Mmmm, L'Etoile, the place where dreams really do seem to come true,' Molly muttered, thinking how much they'd all achieved since they'd met in September.

'You can say that again!' Pippa agreed.

20

From One Journalist to Another

$\mathcal{M}$aria's overnight notes were so detailed, Molly and Pippa couldn't help but be prepared for every kind of question and angle Miss Tangerella might throw at them. As the three girls stood outside Madame Ruby's office waiting to go in and meet Maria's heroine, she was a nervous wreck and in danger of totally losing the plot.

'Will you pull yourself together, Mimi,' Molly said, adjusting her sister's ponytail. 'Anyone would think she's royalty, the way you've gone to jelly.'

'I know! How embarrassing is this? In fact I don't ever remember feeling this bothered about anything in my life. I can't believe I actually pleaded with you to do my hair this morning!'

Pippa giggled, watching the sisterly banter unfold. So that's two weak spots she'd discovered about Maria Fitzfoster now – puppies and journalists! She was sure both pieces of information would come in very useful some day!

'Enter!' came Madame Ruby's voice as Miss Hart's smiling face appeared at the door to welcome the girls.

'L'Etoilettes, may I present Miss Luscious Tangerella of the *London Gazette*.'

Molly took the lead, terrified Maria might be too in awe to introduce herself. 'Molly Fitzfoster, delighted to meet you, Miss Tangerella,' she said, calmly stepping forward to shake Luscious's hand.

'Likewise, Molly. But, please, call me Luscious,' the journalist replied. 'And you must be Maria Fitzfoster,' she said, turning to the brunette version of the first twin. 'I understand you were the instigator and investigator behind this fabulous reveal.'

Maria thought she might faint, but somehow gathered herself. 'It was a team effort, Miss Tangerella . . . erm, Miss Luscious. But I have to say that your article was pivotal to our search and subsequent discovery. It's an honour to meet such a wonderful, insightful writer.' Maria could see she'd said the right thing from the sudden twinkle in Luscious's eyes.

'And that leaves Miss Burrows. It's lovely to meet you too, Pippa.' And she motioned to the empty sofa in front of them. 'Please girls, have a seat, relax, and tell me the whole story from start to finish. Maria, perhaps you'd be good enough to kick the whole thing off?'

Maria blushed and then went into her very best reporter mode, leaving no detail undisclosed. Molly and Pippa were relieved not to have to do any of the talking. It was Maria's moment to shine and, boy, was she dazzling!

'Let's see now . . . no . . . in all honesty, I don't think there's anything left for me to ask. That truly was one of the most comprehensive accounts I have ever been given of any story, Maria. You've practically done my job for me! Have you ever thought of a career in journalism? You have quite a gift for investigation and reporting.'

'Oh my goodness, it would be my dream job!' Maria gushed. 'I'm so pleased you think I might have promise.'

'You have talent, Maria, in abundance. Here's my card,' said Luscious, as she plucked a smart black and white *London Gazette* business card out of her briefcase. 'Should you ever need any advice on your writing, or wish to come up to London for some work experience with me when the time is right, it would be my absolute pleasure. Be sure to drop me an email whenever you are ready.'

'How wonderful! Thank you so much,' Maria exclaimed. This was more of a result than she would ever have hoped for.

'And the announcement about L'Etoile opening its doors to treasure-hunters over the summer,' Madame Ruby said, coming out from behind her desk. 'Should I just email you the details as soon as we've finalised them? We'd very much like the girls' input and ideas for how the "mystery tour" will work best. As you know, we've not really had enough time to talk it through, but we hope to remedy that in the next twenty-four hours.'

'No problem at all, Madame Ruby. I'll get cracking on writing up the girls' story over the weekend and then you can email me bullet points for the announcement as and when you are ready. The only thing I would say is that the *Gazette* always does a special Easter edition and this would be a great cover story for the accompanying magazine, *Gazelle*. In fact, could I get a quick photo of you all so there's an image for them to attach to the story? I think that would work well. Any objections, ladies?'

Miss Hart and Madame Ruby looked at each other and then at the girls. None of them could hide their glee at the thought of having their picture in the paper in connection with such a marvellous story.

'Let's take the photo, but I will have to call the girls' parents to check that they're happy with the publicity before you use it. Is that all right with you, girls?' Miss Hart enquired.

The trio nodded. 'Mum and Dad haven't got a clue about any of this yet. We weren't sure what we were allowed to say, to be honest, so haven't said a word to anyone. I'm sure it'll be fine though,' Maria answered for all three of them.

'That's settled then. If you could gather together on the other sofa then, please – girls in the centre with the two ladies on either end . . . lovely . . . now, say "Rubies".'

'Rubies!' the group chorused, smiling from ear to ear.

'Perfect!' Luscious said, grabbing her things. 'I'll be in touch.'

And, with that, Maria's heroine walked out of the

door, taking with her the biggest secret L'Etoile had ever known.

'Wow!' said Maria. 'I know I keep saying it but what else can you say? This whole thing just keeps getting better and better.'

'I'm very proud of you, girls,' Miss Hart said, as she accompanied them back to class. 'Particularly you, Maria. You spoke beautifully today and earned some well-deserved praise.'

'Thank you, Miss,' Maria answered as they hovered outside their classroom door.

'Now, I still think we keep this quiet from the rest of the girls for the moment. If you can work together and put your ideas in an email to me over the weekend, I'll draft an announcement with Madame Ruby and get it to Miss Tangerella ready to hit the newspapers next week. I'll also write to your parents and explain everything.'

'Thank you, Miss Hart,' Pippa said gratefully. 'Thanks for thinking of us in all of this. I can't help thinking Madame Ruby's reaction might have been different if you hadn't stuck up for us!'

'The less said about that, the better. And if I were

you, I wouldn't keep reminding me about all the rules you've broken, girls – I might change my mind about that punishment,' she grinned. 'Now, off to class, and try to behave as normally as possible. I know it has been an extraordinary term for you all!'

'That's the understatement of the decade!' Molly giggled, and the girls joined their class.

21

Let the Games Begin!

With only one more week of term left, it wasn't too much of a chore keeping quiet and getting back to normal school life. The girls mainly spent their time looking for Twinkle so they could give her a cuddle every spare second they had during the day, and at night they sat up excitedly gossiping about what the world would think of their amazing discovery.

The email had been sent to Luscious Tangerella regarding the plans for L'Etoile's Mystery Tour and the girls' parents had, a little hesitantly at first, agreed to whatever the school needed the girls to do, publicity-wise – thanks to Miss Hart's astonishing powers of persuasion. The first the rest of the school would know about it would be when they opened the weekend's papers when they were home for Easter and read the headlines. Apparently every major newspaper in the country was keen to pick up on the story, once the *Gazette* had run it. It was beyond exciting!

On the final Friday morning of term, Sally Sudbury burst into the Fitzfoster/Burrows room panting and waving a piece of paper in the air. She was so over-emotional, the girls couldn't tell whether it was good news or not.

'Sally, sit down and calm down!' Maria ordered, ever so slightly concerned that Sally had somehow found out about the *Lost Rose*.

'What is it?' Molly asked, immediately sharing her sister's concern. The girls had all felt a bit deceitful at not being able to share their news with their closest friends – particularly Sally. Pippa was worried about how offended Sally might feel when she read it in the papers with the rest of the world.

'It's Lucinda!' Sally announced.

'Oh no! What's happening? I knew this lovely peace was too good to be true!' Molly said.

'You won't believe it. She's written to me to gloat about the following: A) She's definitely coming back next term . . . boo! B) It gets worse . . . she's not coming back to L'Etoile alone. Since she's been in LA, she's become the best of friends with a horror-hog called Lavinia Wright. She's the hideous daughter of a frightful American chat-show host, Tallulah Wright.' Sally almost choked as she said her name. 'Believe me, girls, when I say she's hideous – she makes Lucifette look like an angel!'

'Oh dear. Well, don't worry, Sal – we'll all stick together. You're with us now. I tell you what, why don't we see if we can put in a request to move into a room with four beds next term? That way there'll be no chance you'll end up stuck with those two hideous girls,' Molly offered, and Maria and Pippa nodded in agreement.

'Would you? That would be a total load off my mind. Yes please, can we?' Sally said, relieved.

'I've got to go and speak to Miss Coates before I go home anyway, to see if anyone's handed my iPod in. Can't find it anywhere. I'll try my best to talk her into it then,' Pippa promised.

Sally loved these girls!!

'But wait, I haven't finished. The worst is yet to come! Lucifette's also emailed me saying how she's managed to wangle this amazing audition for the new

Warner Brothers film at the start of next term. Can you believe it?! Molly, that means she'll be up against *you*! You can bet your life she already knows you're up for it and has begun bad-mouthing wherever she can, to try and sabotage your chances.'

Molly looked thoughtful for a moment, and then grinned. 'Yes, but has the little faker had an up close and personal audience with His Royal Highness, Prince Henry? I think not! I can't wait to ram that little golden nugget down her scrawny throat!'

'Oh Molly, good attitude!' Sally exclaimed with a smile. 'I was so worried about telling you that. I thought you'd go mad.'

'I would be worried if I was up against someone who might actually get the part – but, let's face it girls, Lucifette might be the daughter of a world-famous film director and a Hollywood actress, but that's where her plus points end. I'm confident I've got more acting ability in my big toe than she has in her whole body!'

'Well said, Moll!' Pippa cheered. 'Look what happened when she tried to play dirty and ruin me last term. She's the one who ended up with egg on her face.'

'I hear what you're saying, girls, but you just don't know her like I do. She's ruthless if she wants something badly enough and she'll tread on anyone or anything to get her way,' Sally answered, her brow furrowing in concern. 'And don't forget, she's got that evil little witch, Lavinia, on her side now. Talk about double trouble!'

'Sally, I love you for feeling so protective, but you've seen how we Fitzfosters and Burrows operate. Anyway, we've got you on side now so that makes us quadruple trouble. Look, don't worry. I vowed the morning we met Miss Marciano—'

'What, when she nearly ran us over?' Molly blurted out, remembering having to dive into the lavender to save her own skin.

'Yes!' Maria cried. 'I promised myself then that I'd never let that little upstart get the better of us, or anyone else for that matter. I for one am ready for a battle. Let the games begin! Anyway, apart from the obvious, it's been quite a tame term all in all. We'll be ready for a bit of drama after Easter.'

'A tame term!' Pippa squealed. 'It's been pretty scary at times, TTD for one. My stomach was in knots every time I took Twinkle out. And then there are all the good things that have happened, like winning my award and most of all hearing you all perform my song so amazingly. With everything we've got up to, I can't believe I've made it to the end of term – by the skin of my teeth!'

'Are you kidding Pippa? What are you talking about? You are the L'Etoile singer-songwriting talent of the millennium! They'd never expel you. Even Prince Henry was on his feet after hearing "Friends Forever",' Sally said.

You have to remember, Story-seeker, that Sally didn't yet know about Agents Fitzfoster and Burrows and their quest for the Lost Rose of L'Etoile.

'I agree with you, Pips. I don't think it's been tame at all,' Molly said. 'Literally ALL my dreams have come true this term; I've met a real live Prince Charming, who even saved me from my clumsy self; I've landed the audition of my life; I've fallen in love with my little Twinkle and successfully found her the loveliest new daddy . . . and, to top it all, I've finally worked out how to create the perfect curl with hair straighteners!'

Maria rolled her eyes. Giggling, Molly added, 'Only joking about the last bit.'

'I suppose you're right, girls,' said Maria. 'And,

Sally, just think . . . who would have guessed we'd be standing here asking you to be our new room-mate for the summer term? We thought you were public enemy number two not so long ago!'

'Oh, girls! Who'd have thought any of us would be as close as we are? It's like suddenly finding you have two more sisters! Bring on next term. Who knows what we'll get up to?' Molly said, grabbing the other three for a group hug.

'One thing I do know is that I'm going to have to re-write "Friends Forever",' said Pippa, a serious look on her face.

'What? Why?' Molly, Maria and Sally said in alarm, worrying they'd said something wrong.

But Pippa just winked and started to sing:

Ooooh . . . just little old me,
Ooooh . . . then we were three . . . I MEAN FOUR!

And the others joined in:

I can't explain the feeling,
The one that leaves me reeling.

I never thought that friends could be
A second kind of family,

Ooooh . . . this ain't no short-term endeavour
Oooooh . . . you know we're friends forever . . .

the orion star

Sign up for **the orion star**
newsletter to get inside information
about your favourite children's authors
as well as exclusive competitions and
early reading copy giveaways.

www.orionbooks.co.uk/newsletters

Follow  @the_orionstar on *twitter*.

Orion
Children's Books